PUFFIN BOOKS

Editor: Kaye Webb

THURSDAY

No one knew Thursday very well; no one had taken the trouble, with his father away and 'not coming back for a long time', his mother dead, and only an unpleasant stepmother coming and going from his home. Even his name hadn't been properly chosen for him, but had been tacked on to him for convenience by the nurses at the hospital where he was born.

So when he was lost no one knew where to look. His friends Lynne and Nick thought he might have joined a pop group, the school thought he was just playing truant, and strange, countrified Mrs Smith at the newsagent's had the most outlandish, superstitious, impossible idea of all.

Bee, who knew him better than anyone, was just as puzzled; but only she could find Thursday and bring him back – wherever he was, and in whatever torment. And in the end she managed, though it turned out to be a struggle in which she had to risk more than she ever thought she could.

Catherine Storr is the author of several books for young readers, *Robin*, *Clever Polly and the Stupid Wolf* and *Polly and the Wolf Again*, and another Puffin book, *Marianne Dreams*; but with *Thursday* she shows her profound insight into the feelings of young people as well as writing a fascinating story that grafts together ordinary worldly modern life and superstitious old country lore in an unexpected and illuminating way.

For older re

CATHERINE STORR

THURSDAY

PUFFIN BOOKS

Puffin Books: a Division of Penguin Books Ltd,
Harmondsworth, Middlesex, England
Penguin Books Australia Ltd, Ringwood, Victoria, Australia

—

First published by Faber & Faber 1971
Published in Puffin Books 1974
Copyright © Catherine Storr, 1971

—

Made and printed in Great Britain
by C. Nicholls & Company Ltd
Set in Linotype Pilgrim

FOR HILARY

CHAPTER ONE

THEY came round to Bee's house when he'd been missing from school for a week. She didn't know. How should she? Feeling rotten, with a sore throat, swollen glands, a snuffy nose, she wasn't interested in what might have happened to anyone except herself.

'Bee! Come down! Someone to see you!' her mother called from the kitchen. Bee had heard the door bell ring, but it meant nothing more than the milk, the gasman, the rent. It wasn't a time of day when her friends might be expected to appear. Week-day mornings in term time belonged to her mother's life, not hers. She wasn't even dressed.

'What is it?' she called back, expecting nothing, not listening for the reply.

'For you. From the school.'

She didn't understand, but she came down, unwillingly. When she saw the two people waiting for her, she was sorry she hadn't dressed. A man, not young, but interesting-looking. He had a beard, bright brown hair, bright hazel eyes. With him was a woman, young, amused. Together they sat at the kitchen table, drinking Bee's Mum's tea out of the good cups, the pink and gold ones. Bee knew at once that her Mum had liked them. If she hadn't it would have been the old chipped mugs. If she'd thought of them as over-grand, it'd have been the same.

'This is Bee.'

'How do you do?'

'How do you do?'

Bee thought, as she'd thought before, it would be funny if

anyone ever answered this question. She could have said, 'My throat aches and so do my armpits and so do my groins. I've got glandular fever, and I feel lousy.' But that wasn't what you. were expected to say when people said, politely, 'How do you do?' You threw the question back, and that was all that was required. No one really wanted an answer. They only wanted to make a noise that meant 'I am a friend'. Perhaps 'How do you do?' was as good a noise as any.

'Miss Codell wants to talk to you,' Bee's mother said.

The young, amused woman smiled at Bee. 'You haven't the vaguest idea who I am, have you?' she said.

It sounded rude to say, 'No,' but there was nothing else to say.

'I'm the new school secretary. I came at the beginning of this term instead of Mrs McIntosh.'

Since the term had only been going for a week before Bee went down with this rotten throat, it wasn't surprising that she hadn't seen her before.

'And this is Mr Tenterden. He's what's called a Child Care Officer. It's his business to look after any children who need help in this part of London.'

Bee looked quickly at her mother.

'It's not you they're worried about. You needn't look at me like that,' Mrs Earnshaw said placidly.

'Who?'

Miss Codell said, 'It's Thursday, Bee. Thursday Townsend. He hasn't been at school for the last week and a half. We wondered if you knew anything about him?'

'Perhaps he's got glandular fever too,' Bee said.

'He doesn't seem to be at home either.'

'He must be! He hasn't got anywhere else to go,' Bee said, surprised.

8

'That's what we wanted to find out. Whether you knew of any place he might have gone to.'

'No. There isn't anywhere. He hasn't got anyone else, there's only Molly?'

'Who's Molly?'

'His step-Mum. His father married her. She's Mrs Townsend, I suppose, but he calls her Molly.'

Miss Codell said, thoughtfully, 'Yes,' and looked at Mr Tenterden, waiting for him to speak.

'We haven't managed to see Mrs Townsend yet. She doesn't seem to be home much,' he said.

'She's never home,' Bee said.

'Who looks after the boy? Who looks after Thursday, gets his meals and that sort of thing?' Mr Tenterden asked.

'He gets his own meals. He's not a baby. He's sixteen.'

'Where's his father?' Mr Tenterden asked.

'He's away.'

'Where?'

'I don't know exactly. I know he's not coming back for a long time.'

Miss Codell and the beard looked at each other sharply as if they understood what this meant. Bee supposed they must, but she wasn't going to tell what had been told her in confidence.

'There aren't any other children, are there?'

'No. Thursday's the only one.'

'What an extraordinary name, Thursday. How did he come to be called that? Or isn't it a proper name, is it a nickname?' Miss Codell asked.

'It's his real name. He hasn't got any other.'

'Do you mean he was registered as Thursday?'

Bee said, 'I suppose so.' She wasn't going to tell them

9

either that because Thursday's mother had died when he was born, no one had bothered to give him a name like other children. His father had told him that the nurses in the hospital had called him, for want of a better idea, after the day of the week when he'd been born. It had stuck in the Home where he'd been reared for the first six months of his life, and when his father had married again and had brought Thursday back to be looked after – if you could call it that – by Molly, she'd gone on calling him Thursday, not as if he was her own child for whom she'd have chosen a proper boy's name.

'When did you see him last?' Mr Tenterden asked Bee.

'I can't remember exactly. I suppose the last day I was at school.'

'When was that?'

'When was I at school, Mum?'

'Fortnight on Friday. Because you felt bad that week-end, and I kept you home the Monday and Tuesday. Wednesday we had the doctor, and he said to stay here till he did the tests and found out what it was.'

'He was at school then. Because we had a debate, and Thursday did the proposing.'

'Yes, he's down in the register for that day,' Miss Codell said.

'What d'you think's happened to him?' Bee asked.

'That's what we're trying to find out.'

'Do you mean something bad? Do you think he's been run over? Kidnapped? Murdered?'

'Don't exaggerate,' Bee's mother said.

'Boys do get murdered. You see it in the papers. Suppose he'd tried to stop a gang doing something, they might kill him to prevent him talking. It happens all the time.'

'Did Thursday go about with gangs?' Mr Tenterden asked.

'No.'

'Did he go out a lot? I mean, did he go to clubs or coffee bars? Or discotheques or Bingo?'

'No.'

'The thing is, we don't know much about him. Miss Stevens knew you knew him, and thought perhaps you'd be able to tell us something about him, so that we had some idea where to look,' Miss Codell said.

'What sort of thing?' Bee asked warily.

'What he did out of school. The sort of places he visited at week-ends. Whether he had many friends. His interests. That sort of thing.'

'I don't see how that's going to help. How d'you know he isn't in a hospital or something? He might have been knocked down and lost his memory,' Bee said.

'He isn't in any of the London hospitals. The police have his description and . . .'

'The police? What for? He hasn't done anything wrong!'

'Bee,' her mother said, warning.

'Not because of that. The police always have descriptions of missing people,' Mr Tenterden said.

'You're sure he's not in hospital?'

'Quite sure he's not in any of the hospitals round here. If he's in one outside London we'd probably have heard, but it would help if we knew at all where to look,' Mr Tenterden said.

'Thursday wouldn't go out of London.'

'How do you know that?'

'He didn't know anyone except me around here.'

'Didn't he ever go away for a holiday? Mightn't there be people in the country he'd stayed with?'

'No.'

'Tell us something about him. Tell us what sort of boy he

is, what he's interested in. Anything you think might help,'
Miss Codell said.

Bee opened her mouth, and then was silent. She'd really
meant to talk. She wanted to say anything that would help,
but when it came to the point, she didn't know where to
begin.

'Yes?' Mr Tenterden said, encouragingly.

'I don't know what to say.'

'Anything.'

There was a long silence. Then Bee said, 'He plays the
guitar.' She saw at once that no one found this very interesting, but after a moment's pause, Miss Codell said,
'Well?'

'Well what?'

'No, I meant, does he play well?'

'Fantastic. Proper chords and sort of running down
below.'

'Has he had lessons?'

'Just a few. He couldn't afford any more.'

'Are they hard up?' the beard asked Miss Codell across
Bee.

'I don't know. Do you, Bee? Was Thursday hard up for
cash?'

'Yes,' Bee said. She remembered Thursday's jeans, the
ones he'd had for two years, so small for him since he'd
started growing that they'd split right up the back. She'd
tried to mend them, not very successfully. And often he
looked hungry, though he wouldn't ever admit it. She used
to bring him back home for a meal as often as she thought
her Mum would stand for it, but she couldn't do it too often
or Thursday would have seen what she was up to and
wouldn't have come. He was proud.

'He bought the guitar with money from the paper
round,' she said. The paper-round money had to provide

Thursday with the things other children got without having to work. Lately Molly had been away so much, with all the money from the Assistance, of course, Thursday had had to buy everything he ate, everything he wore.

'The paper round! That's another contact we'd better take up. Which shop did he work for?' Mr Tenterden asked.

'Cooper's, on the corner.'

'We'll go there later. Anything else you can think of to tell us?'

'He's clever. Good at school. He gets the best marks in his form at most things.'

'Go on.'

'He's mad about English. Poetry and that sort of thing. He likes history. He doesn't like geography, he can't draw at all, so his maps come out funny. He likes algebra,' Bee said, surprised by this as she always was.

'Anything else?'

'Likes French. He's smashing at French. When he talks, it sounds like the records, proper, as if he really knew it like we know English.'

'Had he been to France?' Mr Tenterden asked quickly.

'No.'

'But the school has an exchange system. Some of your year went over last summer and stayed with French families. Didn't you go?' Miss Codell asked.

'Yes, I did.'

'Why not Thursday?'

'You have to have your partner, the French girl or boy, to stay here first. In the term time.'

'Why didn't Thursday, then?'

'Molly. She wouldn't. So he couldn't go.'

Miss Codell looked at Mr Tenterden again and he looked back.

'What does Thursday do in his spare time? When he isn't playing the guitar?'

'Works, mostly. He does the evening paper round as well. Sometimes other jobs, if they're going.'

'But you see him sometimes, not in school? I mean, don't you?' Miss Codell asked.

'Sometimes. Not a lot.'

'Well, what do you do? Does he take you out? Does he come here, or do you go to his place?' Mr Tenterden asked.

'I don't go there,' Bee said. She could feel her cheeks burning, as they did every time she remembered what Molly had said the last time she'd rung the doorbell of the house where Thursday lived. She had determined then that she'd never go there again, and she'd stuck to it.

'Do you go to the pictures together?'

'No. He doesn't like them much, only Westerns, and I'm not mad about them.'

'Not thrillers? Or comedies? Don't you ever go to them?'

'No. He thinks they're daft. They don't make him laugh,' Bee said.

'What were you thinking?'

'When?'

'Just then. When you said "They don't make him laugh". You stopped, as if you'd remembered something.'

'I didn't exactly remember. I just thought.'

'What?'

'Thursday doesn't laugh. Not much, anyway.'

'Do you mean he hasn't got a sense of humour?'

'Not exactly. That means something else, doesn't it? I mean he just doesn't think things are funny.'

She couldn't explain. She knew what she meant, but it was obvious that they, those two, didn't. She looked across

14

at her mother, who was sitting, looking thoughtful, the other side of the table. Mrs Earnshaw said, 'He knows when something's ridiculous. I've heard him tell Bee about things that happened to him so you knew he thought they were comical. It's that he never laughs right out, like some. You know. Doubled up, fit to burst, like some children.'

'So he mostly comes here?' Mr Tenterden said.

'He's not here a lot. Not more than once a week, if that,' Mrs Earnshaw said.

'Do you meet out sometimes?' he asked Bee.

'Sometimes, yes.'

'Any particular place? Or just anywhere?'

'Different places.' Bee saw that this wasn't good enough. She said, 'We walk about sometimes.'

'So there's no one place you'd expect to see him in if he wanted to see you without being able to let you know?'

All Bee's awareness prickled. She knew that this was an important question. It might even be the one they had really come to find out. It wasn't that she didn't like Miss Codell or this Mr Tenterden, she thought she did, quite. She liked Miss Codell's up-to-date clothes, and her amused eyes. She liked the way both of them spoke to her as if she was their own age, not patronizing or superior. But even so she wasn't going to tell them about Farmer's Lane and the bomb site. She and Thursday had never said to each other that it was a secret, but she knew it was. It was a secret she wasn't going to betray.

She said, as casually as she could, 'He'd probably come round here. Or I'd leave a message at Cooper's for him.'

She saw her mother look at her in a way she recognized. It meant that Mrs Earnshaw knew there was something up. Bee believed she could trust her mother and it turned out that she was right. Mrs Earnshaw pressed her lips a little closer together, and she didn't say anything. Bee looked her thanks, but not obviously. They knew each other very well by now.

'Anything else you can think of that might help?' Mr Tenterden asked.

'Can't think of anything.'

'Then I think we'll be going. We'll see if the newspaper shop can throw any light. What's the proprietor's name, by the way? Is he Mr Cooper, or is he just a manager?'

'He's called Smith. I think Cooper's is just what it's always been called. He's all right, but . . .'

'But what?'

'He's got a Mum and a Dad living there with him. They're both old, they just sort of help out. It's them Thursday gets on with best. I don't mean Mr Smith isn't all right, it's just that Thursday says the old couple are super to him. Really nice, you know. If you saw them, they'd tell you. The other Mr Smith's a bit busy, he won't have much time to talk.'

Miss Codell got up. She said, 'Thank you, Bee. That's very helpful. And you won't forget to get in touch with us if anything else occurs to you, will you?'

Bee said, 'No,' and watched her Mum show them to the door. She couldn't wait for them to be out of the way. She knew what she had to do next.

CHAPTER TWO

SHE thought, at least, that she couldn't wait. She went upstairs to her own room and got dressed. It took longer than usual, because she had to keep stopping and sitting on the side of her bed. Before she had finished, her mother knocked and came in without waiting for Bee to say, 'Come in.'

'And what do you think you're doing?' Mrs Earnshaw said.

'Getting dressed.'

'What for?'

'I'm going out,' Bee said.

'That you're not.'

Bee said, 'I must.' But she didn't sound convinced even to herself. She had never felt so tired. All she had done that morning was to sit downstairs and talk to the two who had just left, and to dress herself, but she felt as exhausted as if she'd swum the Channel, or climbed Everest, or run the Marathon in the Olympic games.

'I don't know what you wanted to get dressed for. All you're going to do is go back to your bed,' her mother said.

'I've got to go out,' Bee said. To her horror, quite without warning she began to cry. She didn't sob, tears just rolled out of her eyes and down her face. There seemed no way of stopping. She couldn't get up, she couldn't even pull up the second stocking she'd had half on when her mother had come into the room. She felt as if she had no bones in her body and no will in her mind; they were all flowing out of her in these feeble, babyish, unstoppable tears.

Bee's mother came round to the side of the bed where she sat. Briskly and gently she undressed her, put her back into her nightie, rolled her into the bed and pulled up the covers, without saying a word. She left the room. Ten minutes later she was back, carrying a tray. She laid the tray across Bee's knees, and Bee saw a cup of hot, milky brown tea, four lumps of sugar, and a croissant, butter, and honey in a little glass dish.

'Mum! A croissant! Where'd you get that?'

'Kummels in the High Street. Bought it yesterday and kept it in a plastic bag for your breakfast.'

'But you never buy croissants! They're terribly expensive.'

'You won't get them when you're well, my girl, don't you worry. Now, not another word till you've eaten something. I'll be back.'

She went. Bee found she had stopped crying as suddenly as she'd begun. She lay back luxuriously on her pillows and drank the tea, very sweet and as hot as she could bear. The croissant was delicious, almost as good as the ones she'd had in France. She was generous to herself with the butter and the honey, and she could almost feel strength creeping back as she ate and drank. Not enough to get up, though. Her head was still so heavy it was easier to lean it on the top pillow than to hold it up. Her eyes were extraordinarily heavy, it was best to let them close. When her mother came back a quarter of an hour later to fetch the tray, she found Bee so deeply asleep that she never moved. Mrs Earnshaw shut the door quietly behind her.

When Bee woke from that sudden, distant sleep, she'd lost count of the day, the hour, even the place. For a moment she didn't remember even that she'd been ill, and she was astonished to find the sun high enough to be making patterns on the floor by the side of her bed. Was it morning? She'd be late for school. Then it came back, and she knew about the glandular fever, she remembered waking on other days, late, like this, coming back a long, long way from those day-time sleeps that take one more completely away from real life than ordinary night sleep ever seems to do. She lay quite still. Until she moved an arm, a leg, a finger, she couldn't really feel her body; she was an observer who could move weightlessly and transparently through space, like the sparkling motes of dust which she could see sliding up and down the shafts of sunlight. She was entirely at ease. No hurry, no troubles. She felt as if she were lapped in one of those curving white clouds which look as if they were made of the softest cotton wool, and on which cherubs in holy pictures ride through the sky. She remembered the tea and croissant breakfast inside her, she heard the whine of the vacuum cleaner downstairs. She felt calm and happy and cherished and *good*.

Then suddenly she remembered Thursday.

In a moment she was back in her body again, not calm, not happy, aching a bit round her throat where the glands had swelled up most. She was conscious that her eyes felt dry and puffy, because she'd cried so much. She wasn't at ease, she was desperately troubled. She wasn't even good, she was cruel and bad because she'd forgotten Thursday.

The vacuum stopped whining, and there were bumping noises as Mrs Earnshaw put the furniture back in place. Bee got slowly out of bed, opened her door and called, 'Mum!'

'So you're awake, are you? What do you want?'

'Come up. I can't shout, it hurts my throat.'

Mrs Earnshaw appeared in the doorway.

'You've slept two hours. It's nearly dinner time.'

'Don't go away. I'm not hungry. Leave it for a minute and come and talk to me.'

'You may not be hungry, lying in bed, but what about

me? I've been working this morning,' Bee's mother said, but she came and sat on the side of the bed, all the same.

'You look the better for that sleep. How do you feel?'

'All right. At least I think so. Mum. It's Thursday.'

Her mother didn't pretend to misunderstand, and say, 'No it isn't, it's Tuesday' as people often did when Thursday's name was mentioned. She just said 'Yes,' thoughtfully and went on looking at Bee.

'Mum, I'm worried.'

'What are you thinking's happened to him?'

'I'm not. I mean, I don't know. But he hasn't anywhere to go, Mum. He can't just have disappeared. Something must've happened to him.'

'You're frightened he's in trouble,' Bee's mother said.

'What d'you mean?'

'Look, Bee. I'm not daft. I know his father's in prison, don't I? You've never said as much, but it stuck out a mile.'

'That doesn't mean Thursday's done anything.'

'All right, girl. You don't have to tell me. But that's what's frightening you, isn't it?'

'Not that he'd do anything. Only that they might try to make out he had.'

'Who would?'

'I don't know. Some of the people at school don't like him. Think he's stuck up. He's shy, doesn't talk as much as some.'

'I always liked them a bit reserved myself,' Mrs Earnshaw said.

'And there's Molly.'

'She got it in for him?'

'She's awful. Always at him about his Dad. As if Thursday could help it. If she could make out he'd done anything, she would.'

Bee's mother sighed. 'Ah! But would there be anything?'

'No!' Bee cried.

'Then you've no call to worry. If he hasn't done anything they can't prove he has.'

'Thursday wouldn't . . .'

'Then what're you worrying about?'

'I don't know where he is.'

'Nor where he might be?'

Bee was silent.

'You don't have to mention the place. Just if you had any ideas. That Mr Tenterden, he's a decent chap. He wouldn't want to make trouble for the lad. You'd best tell him.'

'I don't know. Really I don't. Thursday never went away before. He hadn't anyone to go to. Besides . . .'

'Besides what?'

'He'd have told me if he was going. He'd have said.'

'You haven't been at school,' her mother reminded her.

'He could have come round. He likes you.'

Mrs Earnshaw said, 'He's all right, is Thursday. I can't see him doing anything wrong. You should help them to find him.'

'How can I? I don't know anything.'

Mrs Earnshaw said, 'You know where his father's put away, don't you?'

'Yes. But how'd that help?'

'He might have gone there.'

'He wouldn't. His father didn't want to see him. He never went there.'

'He's never disappeared before, has he? There's always a first time.'

'I promised Thursday I wouldn't tell.'

'When something like this happens you can't always keep promises you made when things were ordinary,' Bee's mother said.

Bee saw this. But she thought of herself having to explain to Thursday why she'd told two strangers about his Dad.

'Mum, can't I get up?'

'If you feel like it, yes.'

'No, I mean, and go out?'

'No. You've been running a temperature every afternoon this week. You're not going out, with this wind, till it's been right down and stayed there.'

Bee recognized authority when she heard it. She swallowed, so as not to start crying again.

Her mother said, 'It won't help Thursday if you get worse. What you've got to do is to get properly well. Then you can start looking for him.'

'Then it'll be too late.'

'Look, girl. If he's been missing a week or so already, another day or two isn't going to make all that difference.'

'You can't possibly tell that!' Bee said.

'And you can't tell it will.'

Bee and her mother looked at each other, sparring partners, searching for weak points. Then Mrs Earnshaw said, 'Shall I go round to Cooper's, and see what they have to say?'

Bee thought. She said, 'I don't know. They're always so busy.'

'I could ask to see the old couple. The ones you said Thursday got on with.'

'Won't they think it's funny you going? After those two have been, asking questions and all that?'

'If the lad's missing, there's going to be a lot of questions asked. Of all sorts of people, all the time. That Molly for one,' Mrs Earnshaw said. She stood up. 'You stay where you are, my girl. If you're not hungry, it won't hurt you to do without your dinner for a bit. I'll pop round to the corner and see what they have to say.'

22

Bee remembered. 'But you want your dinner, Mum. You said you were hungry.'

'I can wait that long. I shan't be more than half an hour at the most.'

She put her head in at the door again a moment later.

'And while I'm gone, you're not to go out yourself. I shan't go without you promise.'

Bee said, 'Promise.' She heard her mother's steps go down the stairs, and the front door shut behind her.

CHAPTER THREE

IT was half past one when Mrs Earnshaw came back. Bee heard her downstairs and languidly got up. She found her mother in the kitchen.

'What happened?'

'Wait till I've got the dinner on the table, then I'll tell you. Nothing to get excited about, anyway.'

It was shepherd's pie, made as Bee liked it best, with little bits of bacon dotted over the potato top, the meat inside mixed with carrot as well as onion, firm, not soggy. She hadn't thought she was hungry, but now she found she was. She waited till her mother had helped them both, and then said again, 'What happened?'

'I saw the old man. He was the only one there.'

'What did he say?'

'He didn't know anything. Knew Thursday wasn't about, of course. They've had to get another lad to do his work.'

'That can't be all he said,' Bee said, dismayed.

'No. But I've got to eat, haven't I? I asked when they'd seen him last. He was in on the Saturday morning, the day after he'd been at school, but he didn't come in Saturday afternoon. The old chap remembered because he should have collected his week's pay, and he didn't.'

The shepherd's pie no longer tasted good. Bee pushed her plate away.

'Then you do think he's ill?'

'I didn't say so, did I? I said, he may have gone away of his own accord.'

'He couldn't without the money. When Molly's not there he has to buy the food.'

24

'And hasn't she been there?'

'She wasn't at the beginning of the term. I don't know whether she was back that week, how could I? I didn't see Thursday after I'd started being ill.'

Mrs Earnshaw said, 'Mm,' and went on eating.

'Did he say anything else?'

'Said a lot, but none you don't know. What a good lad Thursday was. Quite different from the boy they've got now, he said. Said his wife was fond of him. Fond of Thursday, I mean. Said if she'd been home she'd maybe know a bit more. It was her saw Thursday last, that morning, it seems.'

'Anything else?'

'What a quiet boy he was, never talked. Except sometimes to the old woman. What's her name, Bee? He did mention it, but it was an outlandish one, I couldn't get it.'

'I don't know. Thursday calls her Mrs Smith.'

'Where does she come from? Is she English?'

'Sort of. I mean she's not French or anything like that. She's got an accent, but I don't know what it is. Welsh or Irish, something like that.'

'He's as English as they come. West Country I'd say from the way he talks. Doesn't like London, he told me, too shut in and no neighbours, but he had to give up his job wherever it was, and the son offered them their bit of the house when he bought the business, so they thought they'd give it a try. We had a bit of a moan together about the big city. Nice old chap. I saw what you meant when you said Thursday got on better with him than with the young one.'

'Can't I go round and see old Mrs Smith this afternoon? When she's back?'

'How often have I got to tell you ...' Mrs Earnshaw

began. She was interrupted by the ringing of the front door bell.

'Who can that be? It's not time for the laundry.'

'It's Thursday!' Bee said.

'You sit still. I'll go,' her mother said quickly.

Bee could hear from the voices that it wasn't Thursday. Her legs trembled so that she couldn't leave her chair, she felt sick and cold. Someone bounced into the kitchen behind her mother, but for a moment she couldn't see who it was.

'Bee! I've come round for a minute in the dinner break. Gosh, you look awful! I thought you were better now.'

'Sit down, Lynne. Had your dinner, have you? Have an apple while I get the kettle on. You can stay for a cup of tea,' Mrs Earnshaw said. She pushed Lynne into a chair and went on talking. Bee didn't know what she was saying, but she knew why her mother was behaving in this uncharacteristic way. She drank some water and felt her heartbeats slowing. She saw the room clearly again, she felt less sick.

'. . . ready for some work,' she heard her mother saying.

'She must have been terribly bad,' Lynne said.

'Not really. But it goes slowly, the doctor says. We'll let you know when to start bringing round her books, won't we, Bee?'

'Mr Webster's asked whether she's working at home already,' Lynne said.

'Tell him it'll be another week. She's still in bed half the day.'

'You've lost pounds! You are lucky! It isn't even as if you needed to. I'm going to get glandular fever,' Lynne said to Bee.

'You're not overweight,' Bee said.

26

'Of course I am. Look at my legs! Horrible, like a hippo. And Brenda's given me a super skirt I can't zip up. I've absolutely got to lose at least a stone this month.'

'Don't have what I've had. It makes you feel lousy,' Bee said.

'You don't look well at all,' Lynne said. Lynne was large and rosy and cheerful. She was one of Bee's best friends. She was one of those girls no one can help liking, warm, tactless, forgetful; ordinary and pleased to be ordinary. She wasn't terribly bright, but she was full of common sense and good humour. She enjoyed being alive. She sat now at the table opposite Bee, and Bee thought she was like the apple she was munching, crisp and firm and good, with just enough tartness in the taste to prevent it being dull.

'What do you want to hear about? Everyone sent you their love when I said I was coming to see you.'

'Tell me about Thursday,' Bee said.

'Thursday? What happens on . . .? Oh, I see! You mean Thursday. I can't tell you anything, he hasn't been at school for ages, almost as long as you haven't. We thought perhaps he'd got glandular fever too.'

Bee tried to say, 'He's disappeared,' but her mouth wouldn't shape the words without making the shape that meant crying. She looked at her mother, who said, 'Your school secretary was round here this morning, asking about Thursday. It seems no one's seen him all last week, and Bee's worried.'

'Perhaps he's run away. He's just the sort of boy who would suddenly go off without telling anyone,' Lynne said.

'What do you mean?' Bee said sharply.

'Sorry, Bee. I wasn't thinking. Only he is funny, isn't he? Never talks like the other fellows do, or fools around or

27

anything. He's sort of separate. You never know what he's thinking.'

'He talks to me,' Bee said.

'Well, you're the only one, then. I don't think I've ever heard him say more than two words except in class. He's funny. He's different, somehow.'

'That doesn't mean he's funny. He just doesn't talk much, that's all.'

'All right. Don't get mad at me. Only I do think it's funny not to have friends or go round with the other boys like most of them do. He's terribly bright, I give you that. I just meant nothing that happened to him would surprise me because he is different. See?'

'What sort of thing could happen to him?'

'Oh, I don't know. I was thinking he might have gone off and got a job for the summer. He could easily get a job singing. Nick says he's heard him sing folk songs with his guitar, and he's miles better than some of the people they have on the telly. Perhaps he's doing that, Bee.'

'I wish I knew.'

'Hasn't anyone seen him? What about his Mum?'

'She's away,' Bee said quickly.

'Then he's probably with her and they just haven't let the school know. Marvellous tea, Mrs Earnshaw! Thank you ever so.'

There wasn't any more to be got out of Lynne. She drank her tea and left. 'I must dash. I'm going to be late. I'll come again,' she said, leaving Bee warmed by her affection, but more disturbed about Thursday than before.

'Nice girl, that. Who's the Nick she talks about?' Mrs Earnshaw asked.

'They go around together. Nick Gardner. He's nice too,' Bee said.

'Do you think there's anything in what she said? About

Thursday going off singing, or something of that sort?' Mrs Earnshaw asked.

'Not in the middle of the term. And he'd have told me.'

'Suppose it'd come up sudden? Someone heard him and offered him a job, a talent scout, like they have on some of the programmes? A lad'd find it difficult to say no, wouldn't he?'

'I suppose he might have.'

'But you don't really believe it,' Mrs Earnshaw said.

'It wouldn't be like him. Would it?'

'Seems you're the only one can tell,' Bee's mother said. They sat looking at each other across the table, Bee thinking about Thursday, her mind going round and round in circles, not getting anywhere, no help; her mother thinking about Bee first and Thursday afterwards, and later still about other disappearing children.

'I ran away once,' she said.

'Mum! You didn't.'

'I did, though.'

'When? How old were you?'

'Fourteen. Summer time, it was, too. I'll never forget how it rained.'

'Why, Mum? What made you go?'

Mrs Earnshaw said, 'Usual thing, I reckon. Rowed with my Mum. She wanted me to take a job in the village when I left school, and I was set on going to the town. I'd lived in the village all my life. It seemed a long time to me then. There were other things. I was second eldest, and it seemed as if the young ones were always on my hands to be looked for. I thought my Mum wanted me to do more for them than she should.'

'What happened? Where did you go?'

'To Newcastle. Broke open my money-box and took the train.'

'Did you get a job?'

'Three days I cleaned the floors in what they called a private hotel. I don't think anyone had ever cleaned those floors before me, not since they'd been laid.'

'What happened then?'

'My Dad came and fetched me home. I'll always remember. I was in this mucky little room at the back where I slept with two other girls, wondering whether I wasn't going to die that minute what with being tired and frightened and homesick, and the door opened and my Dad walked in. He didn't talk. He wasn't much of a talker, my Dad wasn't. He just said, "Put your things together, the train goes in half an hour." Then he took me home and walloped me for frightening my Mum.'

'What did she say?'

'Told me off good and proper for an hour. I've never heard so many home truths before or since.'

'Then what happened? Did you run away again?'

'No.'

'Didn't want to?'

'Wasn't that. My Mum had cancer – I'd not been told, not till I'd been back a week or two. She died a few months after that, so I had to stay home and look after the young ones.'

'Mum! How awful! How absolutely awful! What on earth did you do?'

'Kept them clean and fed, same as my Mum did. There wasn't much else I could do, was there?'

'Is cancer inherited?' Bee asked.

'Not that I know. And don't you get it into your head I'm dying, or any daft notion of that sort. You needn't start ordering my coffin yet awhile.'

Bee thought. 'Isn't cancer awful, though, Mum? Did Gran have ghastly pains for ages and ages?'

'There's worse ways of going. I don't reckon any of them are going to be joy rides, without you die in your sleep. Your Gran didn't suffer much. Cancer's made out to be a lot worse than it need be, to my thinking. If your doctor knows what he's about, you needn't have too bad a time. My Mum stayed like herself all the while. That mattered to her and all of us.'

'And then you met Dad and had us?'

'Quite a bit later. I had to see your Aunt Ettie out of school first. She was a handful, I can tell you.'

Bee thought about her Aunt Ettie. She couldn't imagine her being a handful. Her Aunt Ettie had five children and lived on a farm, and she was strict with both the children and the animals. Everything in the house ran to order and to time. How extraordinary to think of Aunt Ettie being a bad little girl. She looked at her mother, and thought, too, about her. One knew, of course, that one's mother had been a child like oneself, but one knew it in one's head, one didn't quite believe it. Bee saw her mother like a rock; someone who was always there, had always been there, probably had been born just like she was now, knowing all the things a mother needs to know, doing the things mothers do, feeling the things mothers feel. The thought that her Mum had had to fight to get where she was, had had to make mistakes in order to learn what she knew, hadn't occurred to Bee before quite so clearly.

'How old were you when Gran died?'

'Fifteen, just. Day after my birthday it was, she died.'

'I couldn't possibly look after children now!' Bee said, appalled at the idea.

'Let's hope you don't have to till you're a good bit older,' her mother said briskly.

'Weren't you frightened?'

'Might have been if there'd been time to think. Now, you get upstairs to your bed. You look fagged out, and I've the ironing to do.'

CHAPTER FOUR

How long do three days last? If you're on holiday, or doing something which absolutely engrosses you, no time at all. It's the end of the third day before you've begun to realize what's happening, it's the end before you quite know it's begun. But if you're ill, or unhappy, or anxious – or all of these – three days is eternity. It feels as if it would never come to an end. Bee didn't know how to live through the rest of the week. The minutes crawled. She tried to read, but she couldn't concentrate. None of the television programmes interested her. She slept badly at night, waking up often, fancying she'd heard Thursday, seen Thursday; her dreams were full of anxiety, there was always something she had to do but didn't know about, or something she should have done earlier, and now it was too late. She spent the days wandering restlessly from room to room, or lying on her bed in a daze of fatigue and misery. She couldn't eat. What made it all so much the worse was that she knew this wasn't the way to get well, and she had to get well so that she could go out and look for Thursday herself. It was a black, terrible time.

On the Friday morning, the doctor came. He was unusual as a doctor, because he never made you feel he was in a hurry and couldn't listen to what you were saying. This morning he accepted Mrs Earnshaw's offer of a cup of coffee, and sat in the kitchen like an old friend, which he was. Bee drank coffee and nibbled at one of her mother's biscuits, and tried to look a great deal better than she felt. It was important that he should say she was well enough to go out.

'Is your mother starving you? Or are you on one of these slimming jags?' the doctor asked her. He certainly wasn't slimming himself. He was a big man who looked as if he enjoyed his food.

'I'm not hungry,' Bee said.

'How you can sit there, in front of your mother's parkins and say that, beats me. You're blasé. Terrible in a young girl.'

'What's blasé?'

'Bored by the good things of life. Unappreciative because you've had too much of them.'

'It's not that. Since I had this foul illness I can't hold as much.'

'Is she trying to eat?' the doctor asked Mrs Earnshaw.

'She may try, she doesn't succeed,' Mrs Earnshaw said.

'What's the temperature doing?'

'It was down all yesterday,' Bee said quickly.

'You didn't take it until late,' her mother said.

'Well. It was down then, wasn't it?'

'How do you feel, yourself?' the doctor asked. Bee liked this about him. He wasn't the sort of doctor who told you, by rule of thumb, how you should be feeling, he let you tell him, and considered it seriously, as part of what he needed to know.

'I'm better,' Bee said.

Her mother looked at her, but didn't speak.

'Feel well enough to go back to a full day at school?'

'I don't know. But I'm well enough to go out.'

'Five mile walk?'

'No. Just a little way. Can I?'

'Where do you want to go?'

'Just round, near here. I could do some of the shopping for Mum.'

'I wouldn't advise your carrying home one of those bas-

34

kets of groceries I see your Mum carting back some of these days.'

'I could get the little things. Or just go out for a walk. Please. Can't I?'

'Is it friends you want to go and visit?'

Bee hesitated.

'Or just one friend?' the doctor asked.

Mrs Earnshaw said, 'You visit the Townsends, don't you, doctor? The boy's been missing from school this last fortnight, and Bee's dead worried something's happened to him.'

The doctor said, 'Townsend? Which Townsends are they? There's an old couple in Mafeking Road. It wouldn't be them. Where do this lot live?'

'Over the other side. Springhurst Terrace, isn't it, Bee? The man's not been at home this long time, but there's the wife and this boy Bee knows, Thursday. He's Bee's age, just a bit older. You must know her by sight, though. Hair piled up on top, different colour every time she visits the hairdresser, heels a foot high, and skirts she can barely step in, let alone sit down. You'd think she was a girl with her first money in her pocket, to see her from the back, but when you take a look at her face, she's a woman old enough to know better.'

The doctor laughed. 'It's a description that'd fit more than one of my patients, but I know the woman you mean. She's not the boy's own mother, is she? Second wife, or something. She was keen to tell me she couldn't have had the child unless she'd been married in the nursery.'

'That's her,' Mrs Earnshaw said with conviction.

'What's happened to the boy?'

'That's what no one seems to know. The Children's Officer was round here this week, and all they know is, he hasn't been to school since Friday the week before last.'

35

'Doesn't the woman – the stepmother, if that's what she is – know where he might be?'

'She's not home. At least not when the Children's Officer called. Bee thinks she's away a lot, anyway.'

'Has anyone made sure the boy isn't there, not opening the door? Not wanting to answer awkward questions, or ill, perhaps?'

'Wouldn't the neighbours know? Does he know his neighbours, Bee?' Mrs Earnshaw asked.

'There's a lady downstairs, takes in parcels sometimes. She and Molly don't get on very well, though.'

'Someone ought to make sure the boy's not just lying there . . .'

'Dead?'

'Bee!' her mother said.

'Well, he could be.'

'I'll call round there this morning. Not that I think it's likely that he's either ill or dead, young woman. But I'll see what's going on. Self-contained flat, is it?' the doctor asked.

'I don't know what that means.'

'Has it got its own front door? Did young Thursday have his own key?'

'Yes.'

'Did the Children's Officer get in, do you know? I've met him, if it's Tenterden. Good man. He wouldn't have left it to chance if the boy might still be there.'

'You see, Bee,' Mrs Earnshaw said.

Bee looked imploringly at the doctor.

'I'll go just the same. I'm going in that direction anyway, got an old lady who's broken a leg in the next street. Merry as a grig, she is, you'd think someone had left her a thousand pounds instead of knocking her over in the road and very nearly killing her.'

'Please!' Bee said, as he was leaving the room.

'Please what?'

'Will you tell me what happens? Please!'

'Of course. I want to get you well, and it's not going to help if you're worried about your boy friend.'

'Do you think he really will?' Bee asked her mother directly the doctor had gone.

'I never knew him promise what he didn't do,' Mrs Earnshaw said.

'How soon d'you think he could get back?'

'Not for an hour or so, I reckon, if he's seeing his old lady too. There's peas to shell for dinner, Bee. You could do them sitting down and listening to the radio.'

Bee switched on the radio. She did shell the peas, but she didn't hear much of any of the programmes. At five to one she was half attending to a gloomy weather forecast, when the door bell rang again.

'The doctor!' She almost ran to the door. When she opened it there was Lynne.

'I'm skipping lunch. Thought perhaps it'd do something for my weight. Can I come in?'

Bee led the way back to the kitchen. 'It's Lynne, Mum.'

'Just in time. Sausages and mash and peas. Sit down, we've got plenty.'

'I'm trying to slim, Mrs Earnshaw. I meant not to have any lunch. But if you've really got enough – I must say it looks super. Just a little, then.'

'I wish Bee had your appetite,' Bee's mother said, looking approvingly at Lynne's way with food.

'Oh, no, don't! It's awful, being so hungry. Or perhaps it's being greedy. Only my mum's a super cook, like you, and when I smell what she's got for tea all my good resolutions go west and before I know where I am I'm outside another whopping great meal.'

'Have another sausage.'

'No, I really mustn't. They're marvellous, though. Bee, I've brought you some fudge. I made it yesterday and it's come out right, sort of short and sugary, not like that lot I made for the Bring and Buy sale, when it turned into treacle.'

Bee made herself say, 'Thank you.'

'And I meant to tell you straight off. The other night, I was out with Nick and – has Thursday got a twin or something?'

Bee said, 'You saw him? You saw Thursday?'

'I don't know. It couldn't have been Thursday, because he looked right at me, at me and at Nick, and he didn't know us.'

'Where was it, Lynne? How long ago?'

'Night before last. I'll tell you. Me and Nick wanted to see that film, *Never Look Round*. So we went to the Gaumont, and there was a queue right round the corner as far as the fish shop, and Nick said, let's not, but after we'd gone all that way I thought it was silly not to, so we stood at the end of it, and Nick went in and got some chips, and we started eating them and having a sort of discussion about whether we'd stay or not. You know.'

'Go on.'

'Well, we were still sort of saying should we stay or shouldn't we, when the queue started moving. Quite quick. And then suddenly, Nick said to me, "Look, there's Thursday Townsend!" And I looked, and there he was, walking along on the other side of the road.'

'Go on.'

'So I called out "Hi! Thursday!" but he didn't seem to hear. So Nick said, "Hi, feller!", you know, like they do in Westerns. And the boy, whoever he was, looked straight at us, and then looked round, as if he thought we were calling someone else.'

'But didn't you go after him? Did you just let him go?'

'Look, Bee, we were in a queue. We'd been waiting for ages, and it was moving. If we'd left then we'd have lost our place, and we'd never have got in. Besides, it wasn't Thursday. It couldn't have been.'

'If only I'd been there!' Bee cried. Her insides hurt, she felt itchy with anger and frustration.

Lynne said, 'Look, Bee. I swear it wasn't Thursday. I promise you it wasn't. It wasn't just him not answering.'

'What, then?'

'I don't know how to explain. He sort of felt different. He was awfully like Thursday to look at, but he didn't feel the same. It just wasn't him. Honest, Bee. I know.'

'How could you, across the street?'

'I do,' Lynne said. She sat there, unable to explain, obstinate and straightforward. And Bee knew what she meant, though she didn't want to admit it. If Lynne said that the Thursday who looked like Thursday wasn't Thursday, she was probably right. 'After all, he's not all that unusual to look at,' Lynne was saying, practically. And Bee ached inside even more. She felt she'd know Thursday's shining black hair, falling straight round his narrow, clever face, and the way he walked as if he were in a dream always; from walking beside him she had by heart the way his footsteps sounded; regular, firm, purposive, then suddenly one would falter. It made a pattern of irregularity which was like his conversation, unexpected, veering sideways. It was a pattern which made people like Lynne think of Thursday as peculiar. It was a pattern which haunted Bee's dreams.

'Nick thinks Thursday's gone to America,' Lynne said.

'Why? Why America?'

'It's where he'd go. Nick would, I mean.'

'Thursday wouldn't,' Bee said.

'Why not?'

'It's not his sort of place. Too many people all talking about everything. I know he wouldn't go there.'

'Well, where do you think he is, then?'

'I don't know!' Bee cried. It hurt her that they could sit round the table, comfortably full of sausages and mash, discussing where Thursday might be. He might be wandering about, cold and hungry, too miserable to go back to the cluttered little flat where everything was Molly's and he didn't really belong. He might be in a hospital bed with a broken leg, concussion, loss of memory. He might be kidnapped, forced to take part in some gang's activity which would land him in trouble with the law, prison even. He might be just ill, somewhere; too ill to know what was going on, unable to explain where he came from or who he was. He might be dead, run over by a hit-and-run motorist, lying unidentified in a mortuary. Or murdered by one of these maniacs who killed people without knowing them, just for kicks, and hid their bodies in ditches, where they weren't discovered for months or years. How could they just sit and talk? Someone must be able to do something.

'Are you positive it wasn't Thursday you saw?' she demanded.

'Couldn't have been. I told you, he was different somehow. After all, everyone's supposed to have a double somewhere, aren't they?'

The telephone rang. Bee jumped. Mrs Earnshaw said, 'That'll be Dorothy, she said she'd ring dinner time,' and left the kitchen.

Lynne said, cautiously, 'Bee.'

'What?'

'Don't take on so. He's sure to come back. Lots of boys run away at his age. He'll come back. You see.'

Mrs Earnshaw came into the kitchen. 'It wasn't Dorothy, it was the doctor.'

'?' Bee said.

'He saw that Molly. She's back, it seems. But the lad's not there, and she doesn't know ow't. Doesn't know when he might have left, or where he'd have gone. He just said to tell you, Bee, so you'd know he wasn't lying there ill, with no one bothering about him.'

'Did he say anything else?'

'Now't but that that Molly would be enough to drive any lad from home, that had any sense.'

'Anything else?'

'Said I was to throw away the thermometer and go on how you felt,' Bee's mother said, reluctantly.

'Then can I go out?'

'Tomorrow. Only if you feel up to it, mind.'

Bee said, 'I shall.' Tomorrow she was going to look for Thursday. No one else knew the place where he was most likely to be.

CHAPTER FIVE

Bee got up and dressed and came down to breakfast the next morning, something she hadn't done since she'd become ill. Her father was reading the morning paper over his porridge in a leisurely, Saturday sort of way. Her mother was drinking tea, making toast, writing a shopping list and listening to the news on the radio, all at once.

'Morning,' Bee said.

'Morning, stranger. Haven't seen you this early for a long time,' her father said.

'I'm better,' Bee said.

'That's good. Like to come to the Oval this afternoon? Kent v. Surrey, should be interesting.'

'No, I don't think so, Dad. Thank you.'

'Sit down. Toast's ready,' Bee's mother said.

'Pity. That fast bowler Kent have, he's really something to watch. We don't need to stay the full time if you're tired.'

'Bee isn't interested in cricket any more than I am,' Mrs Earnshaw said.

'Women! I'll drop round to Trev's and see if he's free,' Mr Earnshaw said.

'He'll be free if you tell him why,' Mrs Earnshaw said. She looked at her husband, not exactly smiling, but with a look which Bee knew well. It said love and trust and a sort of amused affection like what Bee's Dad had meant when he said 'Women!' It said, 'Men! Spending half the day watching a lot of other men chasing a ball!' It said, 'Men! Half the things they do seem daft to me, and I suppose half the things we do seem daft to them. But we couldn't get

along without each other. Differences are sometimes fine.'
To Bee that look also meant, 'I'm glad there's another
woman in the family,' and she felt warmed and welcomed
and loving, and glad that she'd been born a girl. Trevor
was her much older brother, living four streets away in a
flat with his young wife, Jean. Jean was expecting her first
baby.

'Marmalade or honey?' Bee's mother asked her, filling
her cup with thick brown tea.

'Honey.' Bee had an idea that honey would give her
energy for the morning's work.

'You need to fatten up. Mum been starving you?' her
father asked.

'No. I wasn't hungry. But I don't want to be any fatter. I
think I'm just right like this.'

'That you aren't. You're scraggy. I don't like scraggy
women,' Mr Earnshaw said.

'You're old-fashioned,' Mrs Earnshaw said.

'Just as well for you, eh, love? But you're dead wrong,
too. Look at the sort of thing people paint. Artists and
sculptors and that lot. All their women have a bit of flesh
on them, and some have more than a bit. Look as if they
enjoyed life. That's more than most of these Little Orphan
Annies do, all eyes and hair and no fronts or behinds.'

'Diddy Bibbs enjoys life,' Bee said.

'Diddy how much? Who's he when he's at home?'

'It's a she, not a he. Diddy Bibbs. She's the absolutely top
model. You see her picture everywhere. She's fantastic.'

'She one of these scarecrows you can't see sideways?'
Bee's father asked.

'She's very slim. She looks super in almost everything.'

Bee's father said, 'Mm,' in a not exactly convinced way.

'There's a picture of her in this week's *Razzle Dazzle*. I'll
show you,' Bee said.

43

'You finish your breakfast before you do owt,' Bee's mother said.

Bee ate. After the second piece of toast she was almost uncomfortably full. She drank much sweetened tea and hoped that this would sustain her. She really did feel better, the glands in her neck had gone down and she could turn her head without it hurting. She hadn't had the hot and cold feeling that means a raised temperature for several days. The kitchen where they ate almost all their meals faced east, and was bright with the sun-filled air and smelled deliciously of slightly-burned toast. Bee looked at her parents, her father reading reports of yesterday's matches in the paper, her mother already washing dishes at the sink, and realized that besides loving them in the way she supposed most children 'love' their mother and father, she liked them. She liked the sort of people they were. She liked her mother's solid, comfortable, active shape, her hair, now more grey than brown, her fresh-coloured face which still looked more of a country-woman's than a townee's. She liked her father, big and very dark, with jet black hair and a long Celtic nose. She liked the way they talked to her and to each other, no pretence and no fussing, leaving each other alone, but caring all the same. She even liked the fact that it was her mother who was the stricter, you always knew just what you could or what you couldn't do with her, while it was not so difficult to get round Dad once in a while. And then she thought about Thursday, who had never sat in any room of his parents' and felt like this, because his father was mostly away doing time, and didn't want to be bothered with Thursday when he was at home, and Molly was the same only more so. And 'home' for Thursday had been a series of dirty little rooms which Molly couldn't trouble herself to keep decent, with an empty food cupboard and often no heating, and, worst of

44

all, no one who wanted him there. Bee loved bringing Thursday back to her home. She loved being able to bring him in without warning, knowing that her Mum would be there when she got back from school, and would, not saying anything, make Thursday welcome as if he belonged there too, filling his plate and asking him about his studies, even sometimes sewing on a loose button or brushing dried mud off his clothes. It was good to see Thursday loosen up and talk more freely. He always did after he'd been with Bee's Mum for half an hour or so, forgetting to sit hunched up on his chair, losing all the hesitation in his talking, becoming relaxed and almost eager, like other, more ordinary boys. That was how he was with her, with Bee, when they were alone together. That was how he ought always to be able to be.

She finished the last mouthful of toast, the last gulp of tea. When she took the cup and plate over to the draining board, she put her arms round her Mum's firm, not very small waist and nuzzled the back of her neck.

'What's that for?' her mother asked.

'Not for anything. Just love you,' Bee said.

'Why tell me all of a sudden?'

'I was just thinking.'

'Well!' Mrs Earnshaw said. She turned her head and gave Bee a rare kiss. She wasn't a person who kissed often, or went in for endearments or expressions of love.

'You going out?' she asked Bee.

'Yes. Can I?'

'Don't go too far. Remember, it's your first time out.'

'I'll go with her as far as Trev's. See she doesn't get into any trouble,' Bee's father said.

'I'm not going that way.'

'As you like, Miss. You go your way, I'll go mine. Any messages for Trev, Mum?'

'Tell Jean they can come round tomorrow, dinner-time if they like. But if they don't want to, it doesn't matter, I'll be seeing them,' Bee's mother said.

'If Trev knows what's good for him he'll come.'

'Don't you tell Jean that. Let her say, he's hers now,' Mrs Earnshaw said.

'I'm entitled to have my opinion, aren't I? If I think your cooking's the best he's likely to meet, I can say so, can't I?'

'Not to his wife, you can't. Now get along, the two of you,' Mrs Earnshaw said. She polished the last cup, shining, on the teacloth. 'Bee! It's nippy, for all it looks so bright. Best take a cardigan. It wouldn't do to catch cold.'

Bee went up to her room and fetched her old school cardigan; fawn. She opened the front door with a sense of adventure. She hadn't been out for over three weeks, it was almost like going into a strange city. But she knew where she was going. Dad would turn right, walk the length of the street, then turn left, pass two turnings, then find the road where Trevor and Jean had their flat. Bee turned left. At the crossroads she turned left again. She walked, first fast, then slowly, because already she was more tired than she'd expected, along the long road which ran parallel to the railway sidings. She knew exactly where she was going and why. She knew the old brick cottages, condemned by the local council, but still occupied by three families at least, on the corner of Farmer's Lane, down which she must go. The lane dipped under a damp, festering bridge, black with smoke, and coated with the soot-caked grass of the railway embankment on each side, and then turned abruptly left under the bricked-up embankment on one side, behind the back gardens of what had once been a row of modest little houses on the other. But it was an area which had suffered during the Nazi war. The little houses had been destroyed in the blitz; some of them had been replaced by a great concrete walled factory, the rest of the site had been left, boarded up and forgotten. Once it had been a place where families had lived and had talked to each other over their garden fences, and whoever rode in the engines pulling the goods trains along the siding had been able to look down on gardens and at backyards and windows where real people lived real lives. Now it was all enclosed and blank and forgotten. The rail track was hardly ever used, Farmer's Lane led nowhere, and beyond the factory there was nothing but a boarded-up area trapped between a wall like a colossal tombstone and the curve of the bricked embankment as it swung round towards the north.

Farmer's Lane was quiet; too quiet for a city street. Bee only half liked going there by herself, in spite of the fact that it was mid-morning now, the sun high above her in a near mid-summer splendour, starlings chattering from the ledges of the high building on her right, the sound of traffic only a street away. There was no pavement, only the polished tarmac of the road. Her feet sounded too distinct, too important, alone on that hard surface, distanced by the height of the railway embankment and the wall of the factory, so that she seemed to be alone in a tunnel roofed by the sky. On weekdays the factory, though it faced away from this side, was alive with noise and activity. Because this was a Saturday, it was still. Seagulls suddenly wheeled overhead, reminding her that the river was only half a mile away. Bee felt very small, in a tall world of walls and chimneys. She was glad when she came to the hoardings at the end of the lane.

The hoardings had the usual advertising posters. There was an enormous one in green and blue, bearing the name of a musical show which had been going for over two years in the West End. There was another, brilliant with scarlet and white, which told the non-existent passengers on the rail track what brand of petrol to buy. The letters of the words were all so big you couldn't read them close to, they looked like parts of houses, trunks of trees, columns of rock. Between the upright of an I, and the immense bowed back of a C, there was a gap in the boards. Through this Bee squeezed as she had squeezed many times before. Immediately she was in a different world.

The place had been derelict for more than twenty years. When the stick of bombs had first fallen, plunging through the middle of the lives of the people who had owned the houses, Civil Defence workers had rescued the living and taken away the dead. Later, any objects not blown to powdery dust had been salvaged, and dangerous, tottering bits of masonry knocked down. The site had been roughly fenced in and left. It had been invaded again soon after the war, when the factory next door had been built, and it had then been used as a storage place for building materials and as a meeting place where the workmen drank tea and smoked and sometimes kicked a ball about. But after the factory was completed, new, higher hoardings had been put up and let out for advertisement, while the space within was forgotten, left to run wild. Since the railway siding was now practically never used, no human eye ever looked down into it. It was an island of deserted ground in an ocean of concrete and brick.

Every time she came here, Bee looked round, anxious, in case someone else had discovered the place. In her dreams she sometimes visited it to find that it had been opened up for building, the hoarding torn down, and great machines with mouths full of grinning spikes, like prehistoric monsters, ravaging the ground. Sometimes in these dreams she was furious, sometimes she could do nothing but weep in cold despair. But today as she slipped in, nothing was changed. The sun shone on her kingdom and it was undisturbed, unviolated, empty and silent. Bee picked her way over the uneven ground to the place where she usually sat, the top of a flight of stone steps leading down into what was now a small open area, but which had once been a below-stairs kitchen or a cellar. If you sat on the second step down, you could lean against the top step, with your feet on the third. It was on the north side of the site, full in the sun. Bee's legs felt weak and shaky, even after such a little walk. She was glad to sit down.

The bomb site was wild. Just now, in the early summer, it wasn't the jungle it became towards August and September, when the purplish pink flowers of the willow herb coloured the place as if it were perpetually in the glow of a sunset, and the long violet cones of buddleia filled the air with the smell of warm honey, which mixed oddly with the familiar London smell of hot soot, petrol fumes and tar. There had been days last year, when the sun had shone really hot, so hot that Bee had wondered whether you could truly fry an egg on one of the few flagstones remaining, and the enclosure had resounded with the hum of the bees visiting one honey-filled blossom after another. She and Thursday, lying side by side in a space they'd cleared of nettles, just by the mound at the far end of the site, had speculated about frying the egg, had wondered where the bees went with their honey. 'Perhaps there's a wild bees' nest in one of the walls. If we climbed up and found it, we could live on it for a bit. Stay here and never go outside at all. I'm sure there must be pigeons' eggs somewhere. We could drink the water in the tank,' Bee had said.

'You'd die if you drank that water. It's filthy,' Thursday had said.

'We could boil it. We'd have a kettle, or an old saucepan. We could make a fire in the downstairs grate.'

The only bits of the original houses which were still standing were up at the railway embankment end of the bomb site; almost the whole of one wall joining the other at right angles. The whole one had once had a chimney breast running its full height, and this had been sliced in half, by the bomb, or by the subsequent demolition workers. In spite of the time which had passed you could still see the remains of the wallpapers on the walls of the rooms round the fireplaces, faded and dirty, soaked by rain and stripped by wind. The original patterns were lost, but faint traces of colour lingered. The one on the top right was a blotched pink, on the left the prevailing colour was green; lower down there was a fawn, brutally cut across by some sharp edge which had ripped the plaster to the brick beneath. The exposed black cavity of the chimney flue cut through the centre of the ruined wall like an irregularly angled scar. Whenever she looked at that wall, and at its neighbour, which showed the outline of a non-existent stair climbing three quarters of its height, Bee felt the nakedness, the awful exposed nudity of that skin which had once clothed a house; more than just a house, a home. People had slept beside that blurred pink wall – Bee imagined it papered with climbing roses, the sort of pattern one could make stories about as one lay in bed on a sunny morning: people had stepped into a hot bath and sat on a lavatory seat under the pale patch where the overhead cistern had hung, they had run up and down the ghostly stairs, they had eaten and drunk and warmed themselves by the gaping fireplaces. What had they felt when their lives were blasted open by the bomb? Inside a house, especially inside a room, you felt safe and protected and private if you chose to be, you didn't count on it suddenly being opened up for everyone outside to look in. Those walls seemed to Bee to expose more than the ruin of a home and perhaps the destruction of a family. They seemed to be giving away the small secret things that people do when they believe they are unobserved, telling the cold outer world who had made faces at herself in a mirror, who picked their nose as they sat on the lavatory, who took sixpence from the change from the milkman, who ate milk chocolate until she made herself sick, who kept a banned book in a drawer and read it under the bedclothes with a torch.

When she didn't look at the walls, Bee was happier. The ground, all at different levels, because, as well as the steps, there were sunk areas where passages had run, and in places, mounds of fallen masonry, had developed a life of its own through the plants which had taken root all over it. It was green and it was growing. On the lower parts of the walls little creeping plants had somehow taken hold in a film of soil and spread spidery fingers over the brick and plaster. Today the buttercups were shining yellow; the whole place had sprung into exuberance since Bee had been there last, four weeks ago; the grass was longer, the brambles had shot up and leafed, the nettles had that deceptive early fresh green which makes them look so much less cruel than they prove when you touch them. There was a patch of shorter grass with dandelions like little suns near where she sat, and she saw that a new crop of seedling trees, sycamore and one little oak, had appeared this year. They grew slowly, these little trees. The first time she'd noticed one, when she'd first found the bomb site two years ago, Bee had expected it to become a tree, a great trunk with spreading branches, in a year or two. But that same sapling was still not as tall as she was, it still looked young enough to need looking after. It wouldn't afford her shade or protection for another thirty or forty years, she now knew. This discovery had made her look at the full-grown trees she passed on her way to school with more respect. Some of them must be hundreds of years old.

Presently she felt strong enough to get up and walk about. This was what she had come for, to look in this place which was so peculiarly hers and Thursday's. But she didn't know what she was looking for. It wasn't him, himself. If he'd been here she'd have seen him at once. She went down the steps to the cracked flagstones, forced apart by weeds, and the small bricked alcove, almost the only place on the site that still had a roof over it, where she and Thursday sheltered when it rained. It was empty. Once, months ago, they had stood there together in a sudden gusty squall, not speaking, just watching the rain coming down, not as if it fell, but as if it were being shot from a turbulent sky. In a crevice in the brickwork here, she had collected odd things she had found among the rubble and the grass; it had become a sort of museum of fragments; little pieces of coloured china, rusty nails and screws, brass bolts, half a wooden door handle, light fittings, a whole dead electric lamp which had miraculously escaped the blitz. Whenever she found one of these sad, useless objects, Bee added it to the collection, almost religiously, as if by bringing them together she could recreate the life that they had once been part of. It comforted her to give each solitary bit of a whole which no longer existed, the company of another in the same forlorn condition. On that cold, blustery day, Thursday had picked up one of the long, pointed nails, and on a soot-darkened brick he had drawn a heart, and inside it a B. Bee had taken the nail from him and drawn a second heart beside the first, an irregularly-shaped thing, because the nail kept slipping, and the T inside it wasn't recognizable at all, it could have been almost any angular letter. Neither of them had said a word. They had not even looked at each other, and the rain had barely stopped when Thursday had burst from their hiding place as if he was frightened that she'd speak, as if he felt actually imprisoned by the shaky lines she had drawn round the symbol for his name. Bee had stayed behind a moment longer to look at their handiwork. She remembered now the glow she had felt, illuminating the dark day, at the first proof Thursday had ever given that he and she were more than friends. Neither of them had referred to it again. Bee had even thought, anxious, that he had avoided the alcove, as if it represented some sort of committal which he didn't want to acknowledge. She had felt him wary for several days after that incident. But they had continued to meet on the bomb site, and after a week or so he had been his usual self. Now Bee looked at the scratches on the brick and wished she could hold Thursday safe and loved in her arms as the crooked letter was held in the heart. She wished she knew that he was well, unharmed, not suffering, alive. She wished she could turn her head and see him as she so often had before, coming towards her across the jungly desert of the ground. Standing in the recess, Bee wept tears as difficult and passionate as that downpour which had driven them there for shelter in the spring of their love.

CHAPTER SIX

BEE didn't search the bomb site that day. Coming up the steps to ground level again, she felt suddenly dizzy and faint, and only wanted to be back home. She hardly knew how she got there. Her legs shook, she felt about ninety years old; she looked at the pavement, longing to lie down on it and die, because that would mean she wouldn't have to make the terrible effort of putting one foot in front of the other. Several times she had to stop and lean against railings, once even to sit on the edge of a low brick wall. She ached, she dissolved, she was in pieces with fatigue. When her mother opened the door to her, Bee was too tired to speak, too tired to listen. She heard her mother say something, and she stepped into the house. Next thing she knew she was in her own bed, waiting for the ceiling to stop shifting from side to side and for the sunlight to stay in one place. She drank scalding tea, but couldn't eat. She slept, woke; more tea, more sleep. The next morning she opened her eyes to a new world, she was no longer tired, she was steady, she was hungry. She couldn't remember what it had been like to be beyond exhaustion until she'd been up an hour or two; just sitting about the house, doing nothing, seemed to be enough to make her tired.

At midday Trevor and Jean appeared. Bee had hardly seen them since she'd been ill; Trevor was never free during weekdays, and Jean had been scared of infection, so they'd only come round to the house after Bee was in bed. Mr Earnshaw and Trevor went off to the pub for a drink before the meal, and Jean came into the kitchen to gossip and to help.

Trevor was tall, nearly six foot like his father, but Jean was small, very blonde, very pretty, and just now very pregnant. She was scatty and cheerful, she teased Trevor, who was inclined to take a serious view of life, and she talked. She talked more than all the Earnshaws put together. She was quite different from Bee's Mum in all these ways, her untidiness and forgetfulness drove Mrs Earnshaw, and sometimes Trevor, wild; but there was something which the older and the younger Mrs Earnshaw had in common. Bee couldn't decide what it was; when she'd first met Jean, as Trev's new girl friend, she'd thought of her as quite unlike the family, but it had gradually come to her that Jean reminded her of her mother, not in what she said or what she did, so much as what she was. She'd tried to explain this to her father once, but she'd got so muddled in what she wanted to say that she believed he hadn't understood at all. His only comment was, 'Different as chalk from cheese on top, but I tell you what, Bee. Jean and your Mum, they both know how to love and how to leave alone.' At the time Bee had felt that this was no more than you might say about any number of people. Later she wondered if perhaps her Dad had known what she was talking about after all.

'Christ, I'm tired! You wouldn't think just walking round here would nearly kill me. It's the heat.'

'It's not all that hot,' Bee said.

'You aren't carrying around a central heating plant like me. I swear this baby's going to be a crocodile, the way he keeps the heat on. Makes me feel like the reptile house at the London Zoo.'

'You keeping well, Jean?' Mrs Earnshaw asked.

'I'm fine, Trev's Mum. Can't say I'll be sorry when it's over though, now. Look at my ankles! I feel as if I'd got football socks under my skin.'

'Put your feet up. Bee, give Jean that chair.'

'Thanks, Bee. That's better. Let's have a look at you. You look as if you'd lost everything I've put on.'

'I've lost five and three quarter pounds,' Bee said.

'That all? I've put on nearly a stone and a half and I feel like the Albert Hall. I asked at the clinic how much of that was the baby and they told me only a quarter, so I'm still going to be huge after he's born. Shan't be able to wear any of my clothes. I can just see myself in maternity smocks for the next ten years.'

'You don't look terribly fat,' Bee said.

'You're joking! I thought I must be having twins, but the doctor says not. Pity, I'd have liked twins. It'd save time. I want to have four anyway, and I'd only have to go through this twice if I had twins each time. I'd like six, really, but Trev says no. He doesn't want any more after this one. At least that's what he says now. He's a lot more scared than I am. You'd think it'd be me that said never again, but it isn't, it's Trev.'

'If it's you something's happening to, at least you know where you are. When it's to someone else, you're likely worried,' Bee's mother said.

'If I knew where he was,' Bee thought. 'If I were with him, so I could see he was all right!' She knew what her mother meant. Like when she'd had that ear infection four years ago, she hadn't worried, she'd just had pain. It had been her parents who'd been scared, having to watch and wait until she was better.

'What's up with you, love? You don't look too happy,' Jean said to Bee.

'I was just thinking. About things happening to other people and not knowing what they were.'

'Someone you know in trouble? Is that what's biting you?'

Bee found she couldn't answer.

'What's happened to your boy friend? Haven't seen you about with him lately,' Jean said, as if she'd guessed.

'Which boy friend?' Bee asked, to gain time.

'Listen to her! Got lots, have you? You've probably packed this one up, then, that's why I haven't seen him around.'

'What's he like? The one you meant? I don't have lots, anyway.'

'This one? Tall. Dark. Gipsy-looking. Smashing, I thought. Good taste, I said when I saw you with him the first time. Walks in a funny way, though, doesn't he? As if he didn't know where he was going to, head in the clouds or something like that. Does he get lost often? He looks as if he might.'

'He's lost now,' Bee wanted to say, but couldn't. Her mother said quietly, 'He hasn't been round here since Bee was ill.'

'You sent him packing, Bee? Had a quarrel or something?'

'No. He just hasn't been round.'

'Just as well till there's no danger of catching anything. I'd have come before myself if that lady doctor at the clinic weren't such an old gloom. "Don't go anywhere near any infectious diseases," she said. And I can't tell you all the other things I'm supposed not to do. "No drugs of any kind," she said, "And don't take too hot a bath, Mrs Earnshaw, not in these last few weeks. Don't stand too long, it's bad for your veins. Don't sit much, or you'll get piles. And don't eat fatty foods, just a light nourishing diet. No alcohol, of course, and not too much tea or coffee. I don't approve of all this milk, either," she said. "It tends to put on too much weight. And go steady on the fruit and vegetables and starch, of course," she said. So I said to her,

"Doctor," I said, "If I mustn't sit and mustn't stand and I can't eat bread or butter or fruit and I can't have baths, it looks as if I'd better stay in bed and eat steaks for the next month. My husband will love that," I said. You should have seen her face! "Mrs Earnshaw," she said, "you don't mean you're still sharing a bed with your husband, at this stage?" So I said, yes I was, and that baby or no baby I wasn't going to change. She was quite upset. "Most un-hygienic," she kept on saying. "You don't want to catch anything just now." "For Christ's sake," I said to her, "what d'you think my husband is? A leper, or something? After all it's his child as much as mine." "Well," she said, "I'm just warning you, you should be prepared to sacrifice your own convenience for the sake of Baby." That's the way she always talks. "Baby", as if it was his name. She's not a bad old stick, but she does have some proper silly notions. My Mum says she reckons as long as I feel well and the baby's lively, I can't go far wrong. What do you think, Trev's Mum?'

'I think you're doing all right, Jean,' Mrs Earnshaw said.

'"Baby",' Jean said, in inverted commas.

'What are you going to call it?' Bee asked.

'Stephen. Stephen Thomas. Stephen Thomas Earnshaw. Like it?'

'Suppose it's a girl?'

'It won't be.'

'It could. Haven't you even thought?'

'Emily Jane. But it won't be a girl. I have a feeling it'll be a boy.'

'Most of us have that sort of feeling, but we're only right half the time,' Mrs Earnshaw said.

'Did you choose the names, or Trevor?' Bee asked.

'We chose one each. First we thought Thomas Stephen, then we decided it was best the other way round.'

'Will he be christened? Properly, in a church? I've never been to a christening,' Bee said.

'You went to yours. Proper row you made at it too. Parson couldn't hear himself speak,' Bee's mother said.

'Did I? Where, Mum?'

'Church at the end of Arnott Grove. Your Dad's Mum wanted it, else I wouldn't have, seeing we're not regular churchgoers. They say if the baby cries when the water goes on, it means the devil's driven out. You cried loud enough for sixty.'

'Stephen's going to be christened. It isn't that I'm religious, exactly. Just I'd like him to be safe,' Jean said.

'Safe from what?' Bee asked.

'I don't know. From anything. Besides, when a baby's born he sort of belongs to his Mum and Dad, doesn't he? But when you have him christened it shows he's a real person. Not just Baby, like the doctor says, but a real person with a name.'

'Saying it out loud,' Mrs Earnshaw said.

'What?' Bee asked.

'What you're doing. Making a bit of a fuss about it to show it's important. If something means a lot to you, you don't want to have it hugger-mugger, all over and done with before you know it's begun.'

'But Mum! You hate fuss. You've always said so.'

'There's fuss, and it doesn't mean a brass farthing, and there's a way of saying things so people know you mean them. Isn't that right, Jean? That's what I meant. Saying out loud, "I'm married for keeps". Or "Here's Stephen".'

'That's right, Trev's Mum.'

'Bee, set the table, will you? Don't stir, Jean, Bee can get round you.'

'Isn't it awful? I'm hungry again. I wonder where Trev and his Dad have got to?' Jean said.

'They'll be back. Dad knows how I feel about keeping Yorkshire pudding in the oven after it's done. It's not one o'clock yet. Bee, switch on the radio, will you? Let's hear about Monday's weather.'

The voice from the weather centre was confident. Warm, sunny spells, mainly dry. Winds light to moderate. Anticyclone. Azores. Moving slowly. Filling up. Further outlook. West. East. Blah, blah, blah. Blah.

'All right. I've heard all I want. You can switch off if Jean doesn't want the news.'

'. . . police messages . . .'

'Leave it on a minute. You never know, it might be something interesting,' Jean said.

'. . . missing from his home since Friday, May the thirteenth, Thursday Townsend, aged sixteen . . .'

'Mum!'

'Sit down, lass, and listen.' But Bee's mother came round to her chair and put a hand on Bee's shoulder.

'. . . slender build, sallow complexion . . . Will any person who may have any information concerning him please ring . . .'

'Mum! Why? What does it mean?'

'Nothing new, I reckon. It's just a precaution. It doesn't mean anything bad's happened to him, Bee. Just means nobody knows yet.'

'That your boy friend? Why didn't you say you were worried about him? How long's he been gone, then?' Jean asked.

'Two weeks.'

'Don't look so upset, love. Having a police message doesn't mean he's dead. Like your Mum says, they'll have everyone looking for him, more chance he'll turn up quick,' Jean said, comforting.

'Do you think, really?'

'Sure. One of my cousins that happened to ages ago. Just went off without saying anything, and his Mum got the jitters, and there were messages on the radio and half the police in the country looking for him, and they found him ever so quickly.'

'How long?'

'Took about three days, I think.'

'I meant, how long had he been missing?'

'I don't know, love. A day? Two, three? Not long. His Mum was a proper old worrier.'

'Thursday's been gone two weeks!' Bee cried.

'Hasn't he got a Mum? What's she been doing all that time?'

'There's Trev and Dad. I knew they wouldn't keep the dinner waiting. Finish setting the table, Bee, I'm going to dish up. And you're going to eat, my girl. If the lad's going to need your help, you've to be fit to give it him.'

So Bee ate, reluctantly. She even tried to join in the family conversation. She wasn't very successful. Her mind kept on wandering away from Trev and Jean and her Mum and Dad to Thursday. Police. The police were looking for him, and she was frightened of what they might find. She almost hoped there wouldn't be any response to the appeal for information about him, in case the news, when it came, was bad, was final. Her body sat in her mother's kitchen, eating her mother's rich roast beef and crisp, airy Yorkshire pudding, but her mind ranged over the city, the country, the seashore, searching for hiding places where Thursday might possibly still be living, and shuddering away from dark corners where he might be found, dead.

CHAPTER SEVEN

MONDAY was all that the weatherman had promised.

'Can I go out?' Bee asked at breakfast.

'This morning I want you to give me a hand with the wash. I'm set on getting the upstairs curtains done, seeing it's a nice day. You help me with them first, then if you feel like it, you can go out for a bit.'

Bee saw the justice of this. If she was well enough to go out, she was well enough to help in the house. But she didn't want to. She felt edgy and restless, she wanted to wander, not to have to stay in one place. She seemed to have woken up a dozen times during the night, starting out of her sleep with half-dreams about Thursday, always a little frightening, never consoling. Her eyes felt hot and swollen. She hoped they looked better than they felt, or her mother would never let her leave the house.

The morning wasn't as bad as she feared. She and her mother worked hard, mostly in silence. Mrs Earnshaw was never one for talking much, and beyond giving Bee directions today, she hardly spoke. At the end of two and a half hours Bee was tired, but she felt better. She began to feel that perhaps after all there might be some simple explanation. The actual physical exercise she had taken had soothed her edginess, and her mother's short practical remarks made her feel at home and saner. When she thought now about going out it wasn't just a wild need to get out and to be doing something, she didn't know what. She knew what she would do. She would go back to the bomb site and search properly, this time, for any signs that Thursday might have been there.

She left her mother ironing in the kitchen.

'I'm just going, Mum.'

'Don't you come back fagged out like on Saturday.'

'I won't.'

'Thanks for helping with the wash. It made a big difference, having you there.'

Bee went out warmed and loving.

The bomb site was peaceful and deserted. Once you were enclosed in it the sound of the city's traffic was distanced, it became a hum which you could ignore, could forget. Today it was hot. The sun had warmed the stones, and the place smelled of hot concrete and warm greenery. Bee began her search. She walked along all the pathways which she and Thursday commonly used: some of them marked out by the original ground plan of the houses which had stood there, some trodden by his and her feet. Her eyes raked the ground. Where there was a particularly luxuriant growth of weeds, she pushed them aside with her foot or fingers so that she could see down to the earth. There were places, of course, which she couldn't reach; one corner was over-grown with brambles, and another, where the two remaining walls met, was occupied by a mound, now grassed over, which was hard to climb because of its steep sides, and uncomfortable to stay on because it was dangerously over-hung by projecting, insecure-looking bits of masonry. But over the rest of the area, Bee went. She was looking for an object, a sweet-wrapping paper, a button, a shred of stuff caught on a bramble, a pencil, a cigarette stub, a shoe lace, anything that would tell her that Thursday had been there recently. She didn't know how she would recognize that anything she found belonged to Thursday. She could only look, and hope that whatever she found might have some stamp of his personality which she couldn't fail to know. But she searched the whole site and searched in vain. All she found was evidence of the year's new growth, the heartless, persistent miracle of the seeding, the leafing and flowering of the season's weeds. Thursday had left no signs on the ground. He might never have been there at all.

Bee came back to her seat on the second step of the flight down into the earth. She now felt tired. Down here, cut off from the wind, it was very warm and quiet. She had wearied herself by her intensive pursuit of something that didn't exist, and she was glad to lean her head on her arms on the top step, and to let herself relax in the heat and the silence. Two early butterflies flew past her in a complicated dance pattern; from high on one of the ruined walls a blackbird suddenly let forth a piercing, triumphant call. Bee was exhausted. Her eyelids wouldn't stay up, and without knowing where she was going, she slid towards sleep. She heard the blackbird call again, and the throb of a distant plane crossing the city; she tried to remember where she was and what she had come there for, but it was too much effort. She couldn't lift her heavy eyelids, she couldn't raise her over-weighted head. She sank, fathoms deep, into unconsciousness. The butterflies danced round her, the nettles trembled, beyond the hoardings the tide of traffic ebbed and flowed, and within the little space, Bee slept.

She woke suddenly and confused. She had dreamed, with extraordinary intensity, that she saw Thursday. He was standing quite close to her, and he was saying something to her, asking her, she thought, for help, but she couldn't hear what he said. She put out her hand to touch him, and found there was a wall between them, an invisible, a glass wall, so that she could only see, she couldn't hear or feel him. She wanted to tell him that she would do what she could, but he couldn't hear her voice. She talked louder. He still couldn't hear. She tried to shout, but the dream took her voice and carried it away, so that with all the straining she could not make enough sound to penetrate the wall. At last, as if he were resigned to their separation, Thursday looked away from her, and she knew that he saw something she could not see and that he was frightened by it. She saw him move, first slowly, then faster, away from the unseen danger, and then, in the illogical way of dreams, he was out of sight. She could hear him, but she couldn't see him any longer, and the threat, whatever it was, grew stronger and closer. She tried to scream out his name, 'Thursday!' but no sound came from her aching throat. The only sound was the sound of footsteps, hollow, echoing, loud at first, then fading, retreating into the distance, and carrying hope with them. They were regular footsteps on a hard surface. One, two, one, two, one, two, one, two, one . . . There had been a hesitation, a sidestep. A foot dragged on the ground instead of a step firmly taken. They were Thursday's footsteps. They were passing now, on the other side of the wall. They were diminishing along the road. Thursday was going away, he was leaving, he was gone.

Bee was on her feet before she was properly awake. She nearly fell, her leg had gone to sleep, she couldn't stand, it was agony to put her weight on it. And she could still hear those footsteps. Getting up suddenly had made her dizzy, she didn't know if she was still in the dream or awake. She stumbled, half crying with the pain of her numbed leg, towards the hoarding, catching her clumsy feet in stones, her skirt in brambles, tearing obstacles aside with her hands, fighting to reach the road. She thrust herself through the gap in the boards and fell into Farmer's Lane. In the vaulted dome of her skull echoed the beat of those footsteps, the rhythm of the interrupted one, two, one, two, the syncopation, the irregularity of Thursday's passage through life.

Because she knew that no one else could walk just like that, she threw herself through the gap in the boarding, confident that Thursday would be there.

The lane was empty.

She couldn't believe it. She looked first towards the open end, the way that led back to the other streets, her home, his lodging. Then back to the closed end, the embankment, the high grey wall under the railway track. There was no one. The lane was deserted. She stood still for a moment, listening, and believed that she heard the pattern of Thursday's feet dying into the distance, further and further away until she couldn't distinguish the tiny sound against the background drone of traffic. Her own heart beat was louder in her ears. In spite of this, she began to run. She ran towards the railway bridge, where the lane curved under the track to join a proper road beyond. There was no one in sight at the bend. Her running steps were twice as loud and echoing under the dank bridge. She came out into the brilliant sunshine on the other side dazzled, and looked up and down the long straight road. It wasn't empty. There were several people walking on the pavements, two parked cars, a delivery van. But Thursday was not there.

She was too much bewildered to think clearly what would be the most sensible thing to do. If she had really heard Thursday's footsteps, he must have come into this road, Farmer's Lane didn't lead anywhere else; but here he might have turned left or right, back towards Bee's home or right towards the High Street. And there were turnings off the long road, he could have gone up any of those. The steps Bee thought she had heard hadn't been hurried, but they hadn't been slow. If she knew in which direction to run, she could still hope to catch up with him. But he could have gone either way, she didn't know how to hope to reach him. And like a blow it struck her that he hadn't waited for her when she called out to him, that it was as if he didn't want her to find him. He might even be hiding from her here, behind one of those parked cars, inside one of the little houses, which, because their windows were thrown open to the summer warmth and sun, seemed to be staring at her distress with wide, unsympathizing eyes. Bee sobbed. She turned towards her own home, not because she'd calculated that Thursday was more likely to go that way, but in a sort of instinctive longing for the more familiar path. She wasn't running now, she walked. She hardly had the strength even for that.

At the T-junction where her road turned off Brigg Street, she crossed the road and meant to go straight home. Then she saw the small sign, TOBACCONIST AND NEWSAGENT, which hung outside Cooper's shop, one turning further on. It was another place Thursday might possibly visit. She went in.

Old Mr Smith was the only person in the shop. He put down the paper he was reading when Bee came in and smiled at her.

'Well now, m'dear! Haven't seen you for a year, it seems like. Are you better, now? You've been quite bad, seemingly?'

Bee couldn't wait to answer this. She said, 'Have you seen Thursday?'

'Not just lately, m'dear. I told your mother, he was in here a couple of weeks ago ... What is it then? You feeling bad?'

Bee said, 'I'll be all right,' but her voice sounded odd, and the shop swung about her. Old Mr Smith opened the glass-topped door behind him and shouted, 'Arianwen!' then came round the counter and half carried Bee into the little room at the back of the shop. She was put on to a chair, there was a glass of cold water at her lips, but she couldn't

67

drink. People were talking over her head, but their voices were like the buzzing of insects, they made no sense. She leaned her head back and shut her eyes. She wished she were far away and need never come back to have to bother to find out what was going on and what they were talking about. She felt it would be agreeable to be dead.

Gradually the world around her settled down, she dared to open her eyes. The noises became words she could understand. Old Mr and Mrs Smith were standing looking at her, speaking about her. '. . . go and fetch her mother,' Mr Smith was saying, and old Mrs Smith replied, 'Leave her awhile yet. She's coming back. See, her eyes are open. What was you saying to her, then, that gave her such a turn?'

'I was saying we hadn't seen her for quite a time. Any reason why that should worry her, then?'

Bee tried to tell them that it wasn't anything that had happened since she'd come into the shop, but she still couldn't speak. She shut her eyes again. She could feel that the two old people were sitting on their chairs looking at her. Presently the shop bell tinkled, and she heard Mr Smith get up and go into the front. The bell tinkled again, and immediately again. There must be quite a stream of customers. She heard voices, the steady rumble of conversation. Her head cleared and she opened her eyes again. Old Mrs Smith was still sitting and looking at her.

'Was you feeling better, then?' she asked. She had a curious way of speaking, lilting, as if at any moment she might take off into song. She was a tiny old lady, with a long straight nose and uncountable fine wrinkles engraved in the skin of her face like the shading in a black and white drawing. In spite of the fact that she was so old – about seventy, Bee thought – her hair wasn't yet completely white or even grey. You could see that it had been black.

Her curved, delicate eyebrows were still dark and her eyes bright underneath them.

'Much better. I'd better go home,' Bee said.

'Will your Mam be wondering where you are? Did you should've been back this long time?' the old woman asked.

'No.'

'Then stay for a while yet. I'll make you some tea.'

There was an electric kettle on a table by the window. It seemed strange to Bee to see old Mrs Smith plug it into the wall socket, as if using modern equipment like this came to her naturally. With her odd country accent, and her looks, and the air she had of not belonging to the general run of old ladies, Bee would have expected her to refuse to have anything to do with electricity, and to insist on boiling an old-fashioned black kettle on an open fire. Possibly even a cauldron over a stick and faggot fire out of doors. But old Mrs Smith seemed perfectly at home with her son's up-to-date methods, and the tea she made was ordinary Brooke Bond tea in a bulging brown teapot, and they drank it out of white china cups with saucers and teaspoons in the usual manner. There were even petitbeurre biscuits out of a grocer's packet. Bee began to feel her usual self again, until Mrs Smith, after their second cups, said, 'What was it troubled you, my soul?'

The cup in Bee's hand clattered on its saucer. She put it down.

'Is it the lad?'

Bee nodded.

'You haven't seen nor heard of him? Not hide nor hair, not an eyeblink nor a footfall?'

Bee hesitated.

'He's vanished off the face of this earth entirely?'

'No!' Bee cried.

'I wasn't saying he'd met his death, my heart.'

'What do you mean?' Bee asked, trembling.

'Nor more than I said. That he'd vanished.'

'You said off the face of the earth.'

'Does he have to be wandering on the surface of the globe like the Jew that had no pity on that poor man carrying the cross he was to die on?'

'I don't understand what you're saying. If he isn't on the earth, where is he, if he's still alive? You don't mean he's at sea?'

'Not on, child. Not on the earth. In.'

'You mean buried?' Bee cried.

'Do you not know what I'm saying, truly? Must I've to say it aloud, that shouldn't be spoken? I thought you'd jump to my meaning when I'd said as much,' old Mrs Smith said.

'I haven't any idea what you're talking about,' Bee said.

Mrs Smith looked round the small room. She got up and shut the window. She pushed the door into the front shop with her foot to make sure it was shut fast. She sat down in a chair near to Bee's and leaned across to her.

'They've took him,' she said in a whisper.

'Who?'

'They. Them that's everywhere. The good people.'

'The *good* people? How can they be good if they've kidnapped Thursday?'

'Don't speak so loud. Surely you've heard of the good people?'

Bee stared at her.

'I'm to blame. I should've known they'd be after him. The signs were there, and I never read them,' Mrs Smith said.

'You mean kidnapping?' Bee asked. She didn't understand Mrs Smith's language, she wanted to hear what was said in different words, words which had some meaning for her, which belonged to ordinary life.

'Not that. Taken, like I said. Exchanged, that's the usual way of it.'

'We ought to tell the police,' Bee said.

'What's police got to do with it?'

'But if he's been taken – you don't mean he wanted to go? Against his will, you mean?'

'At his age they'd tempt him. Get him to start along the path with them, then shut the door behind. Once he's in, he stays.'

'He wouldn't. Thursday wouldn't. He'd try to escape.'

'He wouldn't know to escape. That's their strength. Remember, to him it's only hours gone by. Minutes, maybe. He doesn't know about you grieving out here in the cold. To him it's only a moment that he's playing at the feast.'

'What feast? What d'you mean, it's only a moment? If you know where he is, all about the people who've taken him, why don't you do something? Who are they? Where is he? Why don't you explain?' Bee cried.

The old woman was silent, looking at her. Bee had the feeling that she was expected to make sense, without any more help, of this jumble of nonsense. She wondered wildly, for a moment, if old Mrs Smith was speaking in some sort of code, if there were a message here which she ought to be able to receive. She couldn't. It all sounded mad. But Mrs Smith didn't look mad at all. She even sounded confident, as if she really knew where Thursday might be. She said now, in an even lower whisper, 'The good people. The little people.'

Outraged and furious, Bee said, 'Fairies!' Or rather she began the word, but didn't finish it. Two things happened at once. Mrs Smith put a hand over her mouth, and the door opened and old Mr Smith came back. 'Feeling better?' he asked Bee. 'Give me a cup of your tea, Arianwen, my mouth's dry with hearing so much talk.'

'I must go,' Bee said. Mr Smith was for persuading her to stay, but his wife seemed almost as anxious to say good-bye as Bee was to leave. 'Her Mam will be wondering where she's wandered. Let her go, she'll come again another day,' she said, though Bee herself, angry and humiliated, felt that she could never come there again. She'd been tricked, spoken to as if she were a baby, or it was a joke, a cruel one she couldn't forgive. Bee hated the old woman. The only extraordinary thing was that old Mrs Smith didn't look as if she'd been joking or as if she thought Bee childish enough to be told fairy stories. She looked as she always did, lively and composed. She paused before opening the door out to the road and looked at Bee with those bright dark eyes. 'You've not to speak of them if you don't want them to work against you,' she said with complete serious-ness, then quickly pushed Bee out into the sunny street.

CHAPTER EIGHT

BEE sulked.

'What's troubling you? Is it the lad?' her mother asked, at breakfast the next day.

'Sort of. Not exactly.'

Mrs Earnshaw waited for a time. Then she said, 'You can talk or not. I'm not worried.'

Bee said, 'It's that old Mrs Smith. She's barmy.'

'How? I thought you liked her.'

'I did. Till yesterday.'

'What happened yesterday? I didn't know you'd seen her.'

'She talked about Thursday.'

'What did she say?'

'It's so silly. She must think I'm daft.'

'What did she say?' Mrs Earnshaw said again.

'Said he'd been taken.'

'Who by?'

Bee could hardly bring herself to say it. 'By the fairies. Honestly, Mum, she must think I'm wanting. Whoever would believe a tale like that?'

Mrs Earnshaw said, seriously, 'She might. Doesn't she come from the country?'

'Yes. But so do you. And Dad. You wouldn't ever tell tales like that. She's crazy.'

'You haven't ever lived in the country, Bee,' her mother said.

'But, Mum! You don't mean you believe that sort of rubbish?'

'What sort of rubbish?'

'Fairies. Being stolen, and that. It's babies who'd believe in that. You don't, do you, Mum?'

Mrs Earnshaw said, 'I never had any use for fairies. There's enough going on in the world without them. Science and atom bombs and people with plastic hearts and everything. The more they discover, the more there is we don't properly know about. That's about as much as I can follow. Fairies is something extra, another way of saying the same thing, I shouldn't wonder. Anything we don't know properly about is fairies, I reckon. You shouldn't be too hard on the old lady, Bee. When she talks about her fairies, all she's saying is that she doesn't rightly understand, isn't that it?'

'But if she says Thursday's with the fairies, Mum? What's that supposed to mean?'

'My gran said she'd seen them,' Mrs Earnshaw said.

'Who? The fairies?' Bee asked, unbelievingly.

'That's right.'

'But you didn't think she really had?'

'My grandad used to say it must've been after she'd had a couple on a Saturday night.'

'And was that it? Was she a bit tight?'

'My gran never drank a drop, except at Christmas and birthdays, like.'

'Then what did she see? I mean, why did she think she'd seen fairies?'

'There's times you think you've seen one thing, then when you go close and look it's something other. The other day I went to pick up a new penny in the road, and when I got there it was one of those metal tabs you get on bottles. Or I've thought I saw someone I knew, and then when I took another look it wasn't. The seeing's one thing. Knowing what you've seen's something different.'

'The other morning I woke up a bit muddled and I

74

thought I was in a country all snow and hills, and it was only the bedclothes. I'd got my knees up and they made mountains. I know,' Bee said.

'That's right.'

'But old Mrs Smith can't have seen anything.'

'How'd you know? Did you ask her?' Mrs Earnshaw said.

'No.'

'Then you don't know what she saw or didn't see.'

'I'll go and ask her this morning,' Bee said.

'If it's something she heard she should tell the police, now it's in their hands.'

'What d'you mean?' Bee asked quickly.

'If anyone's been talking of him, saying they've seen him or heard of him, it's for the police to look into it now,' her mother answered.

'Not if you thought you'd heard him?'

'How, heard him?'

'Walking,' Bee said.

'Walking? What do you mean, lass?'

'Walking. His footsteps. I thought I did, and then he wasn't there.'

'Where? Don't fret. Where did you hear him walk?'

'Round here. The other side of a wall, then when I got there, he'd gone.'

'Could you tell for certain it was him?' Mrs Earnshaw asked.

Bee said, 'No. I suppose not.' It wasn't true, but she couldn't tell her story to the police. It would feel like a betrayal of Thursday. He never talked about himself to anyone except to her. He never said to her, 'Don't tell,' but she knew that he trusted her not to. One of the things that hurt most about this disappearance was that he hadn't told her he was going. Bee couldn't wish that he was in danger

75

in order to comfort her hurt feelings, and yet sometimes she did. Sometimes she imagined him ill, wounded, kidnapped, dead, and while part of her suffered for what he might be suffering, another side of her nature said, 'At least he didn't leave you by choice, without a word.'

'D'you think the police know anything yet?' she asked.

'How would I know? Could be.'

'Would they tell anyone? The police, I mean.'

'They'd tell whoever reported him missing. The school, I reckon that'd be. I can't believe that Molly had much to do with it.'

'I could go and see Miss Codell. She was all right.'

'Bee,' her mother said.

'What?'

'Don't set your hopes too high, lass. When there's a message like that on the radio, there's all kinds of folk writing in saying they've seen the one that's missing, and the most of them haven't done anything of the sort. There's always a hundred answers that don't help, for one that does.'

'But there can't be so many boys like Thursday!'

'No, but there's a sight of folks wanting to draw attention to themselves, and any way's better than none, as they see it.'

'You mean they'd say they'd seen Thursday when they hadn't at all?'

'Persuade themselves they'd seen something like the lad.'

'I'll go and see if they've heard anything at the school.'

It was extraordinary, it felt all wrong, to approach the school building in the middle of the morning. It wasn't like going there in the holidays, which she'd done before now, either, because then the whole place was quiet and deserted, and you were conscious that your friends were out in the streets behind you, that the school building was resting, as it were, from the term's frantic activity. Today the windows were open, there was a buzz of voices coming across the hot ground. Bee could see heads moving about, she could smell the dinner being cooked in the kitchen. She felt enormously alone, sad, as if she'd been pushed out of her place in the hive, and strange. It was strange not to be able to go in through the cloakroom doors, which were locked, to have to use the front door as if she were a visitor. It was strange to be the only person walking up the wide stairs, and to have no temptation to talk, which was forbidden there, because she had no one to talk to. It was extraordinary to knock at the secretary's door without the customary sinking of the heart which went with obeying a summons to the headmaster's room. She went into Miss Codell's little room feeling like a different person. Not Bee, who belonged in that room only when she'd broken a rule, but who would have come then direct from the strength and comfort of her friends.

The amused eyes didn't recognize her. 'Yes?' Miss Codell said.

Bee said, 'I'm Bee. Bee Earnshaw. You came round to our house last week. About Thursday Townsend.'

'Of course! I knew I'd seen you before, but I couldn't think when. Are you back in school, then?'

'No. I came in to see you,' Bee said.

'What can I do for you?'

'It's Thursday. There was a police message on the radio. I heard it, Sunday. Mum said you might know if there'd been any answers. If anyone had phoned in to say they'd seen him, or anything like that.'

'I haven't heard anything, but I wouldn't. It'd be Mr Tenterden who'd get the message from the police, if they had any news.'

'How would I ask him?' Bee said.

'I'll ring him now,' Miss Codell said. She pulled the telephone towards her and dialled. 'She knows the number by heart,' Bee thought, 'perhaps they're friends. Perhaps they're in love with each other, they're going to get married.' She examined Miss Codell with her eyes, watching for a sign that Miss Codell loved Mr Tenterden. But the conversation was matter-of-fact and brief, and, Bee could feel, disappointing. She knew what to expect when Miss Codell said to her, 'I'm sorry, Bee. The police say that nothing useful has come in so far.'

'Has there been something, then?'

'One or two messages they followed up that turned out to be no good.'

'Didn't they say anything else? Hasn't anybody seen anything?'

'Would you like to go down to the police station and talk to them yourself?'

'Could I? Would they tell me everything that's happened?'

'You might be able to help them. You might know where they should start looking.'

Bee's eagerness died. She'd thought only of the questions she would ask, not of what the police might ask her. There was too much she couldn't say.

'Will you tell me if there is any news?' she asked.

'Of course I will.'

'Thank you very much.'

'You won't stay and have a cup of coffee with me? I think you rate as a visitor today.'

Bee was surprised into agreeing. She was put into the visitors' chair, and not allowed to help. She looked at Miss Codell's short, pale fair hair, and her springy eyebrows – they were what made her look always amused – and thought she'd never seen anyone so very much alive. She wasn't pretty, her face was too full of bones for that, but she looked interested and interesting, Bee decided. She'd just got the cup of steaming coffee in her hand, when the door that led into the headmaster's study opened suddenly. Bee almost spilt her coffee when Mr Stanton himself came in.

'Antonia! You aren't doing your duty. I smelled coffee, and you haven't offered any to me,' he said. Then he saw Bee. 'I beg your pardon. I hadn't realized Miss Codell was entertaining.' He almost disappeared again.

'Mr Stanton! Don't go. I've made a cup for you. I was going to bring it in,' Miss Codell said.

'Really? That was good of you. I shan't refuse, I'm exhausted.' He looked piercingly at Bee. 'Are you a visitor? Somehow your face seems familiar. I feel as if I should have been teaching you two minutes ago. You'll have to forgive me if I've made a mistake.'

Bee said, 'I'm Bee Earnshaw, Mr Stanton. I'm in Lower Five K, only I've been away with glandular fever for the last three weeks.'

'I see. This is an informal visit. When are you being allowed to come back to us officially?'

'Bee was asking about Thursday Townsend, and I thought it would be all right to give her some coffee before she went home,' Miss Codell said.

'Of course. Quite right. You'll forgive me if I take my cup into my own room and get on with some correcting,' Mr Stanton said. When the door shut behind him, Bee heard Miss Codell's sigh. 'How extraordinary, she wasn't sure he mightn't be cross at my being here,' she thought. She saw Miss Codell with different eyes. On the day she'd come to Bee's house to ask after Thursday, she'd seemed on the far side of grown up, beyond that unthinkable frontier, but today she seemed young enough to be one of Mr Stanton's pupils rather than one of his staff. Bee realized suddenly that she wouldn't ever wake up one morning and discover that she was grown up, that she'd stopped being a child. She had a vision, sitting there in the school secretary's room, drinking instant coffee, of the creeping progress of each one of us towards understanding. She knew that the age of people in years is only a delusion, that no one is all of a piece, we grow by uneven steps, and our outward showing often doesn't agree with our inner fears. She saw that people have to learn their jobs as children learn their lessons. Miss Codell was learning how to be a school secretary; Trev and Jean were learning to be married. She supposed that Jean would have to learn to be a Mum. It made her feel older herself, to have seen all this, and more hopeful. If other people could learn, so could she.

'He didn't mind my being here,' she said.

'I didn't really think he would. He's very nice to work for,' Miss Codell said.

'Are you going to stay?'

'Yes, if they'll keep me. I came as a temporary, until they could get someone else, when Mrs McIntosh left suddenly, and I was terrified at first. But so far I think it's all right. I shall stay for the term, anyway, then they'll decide.'

'I hope you stay,' Bee said.

'Thank you.'

'I couldn't help hearing. Is your name Antonia?' Bee said, daring.

'Yes. It's a family name.'

'Were your ancestors called Antonia, do you mean?'

'They were mostly called Anatalia. They weren't English, you see.'

'Aren't you English?' Bee asked.

'I suppose so. I was born here. My father came here from Hungary when he was a young man.'

'Do you feel Hungarian?'

Miss Codell laughed. 'Sometimes, terribly. When I don't

80

like what people do, I feel "I'm Hungarian. You bloody English."' She stopped suddenly. 'I'm sorry. I shouldn't have said that.'

'I don't mind. I think it must be super to be something like Hungarian. Sort of exciting.'

'I didn't mean sorry for that. I meant I shouldn't have said bloody. Not at school. Mr Stanton wouldn't like it.'

'I suppose not. Though heaps of people do say it. Even on television.'

'But not on schools programmes.'

'Well, it's all right, anyway. I mean, I do know how people talk ordinarily. Go on about feeling Hungarian.'

'Sometimes I feel "You bloody foreigners" and then I'm being English.'

'I wish I were two different things like that.'

'You probably are, only you may not realize it.'

'How do you mean?'

'Well, for instance. You belong to your family, and you don't. You'd be furious if you heard someone outside criticizing them. That's when you belong. But sometimes you'd be criticizing them, then you're on the outside yourself.'

Bee said, 'Yes, I see.' She thought about this. It fitted in with the understanding she'd reached five minutes earlier about being grown up. She saw that it might be possible to be both grown up and a child at the same time, so that you moved from feeling 'bloody grown-ups' to 'revolting children' and back again, not firmly on either side of the dividing line. She saw suddenly that you can be more than one thing at a time and yet be all of one piece, your you-ness making a whole person instead of a lot of little bits.

'You're looking very serious, Bee,' Miss Codell said.

'I'm thinking.'

'What are you frightened of? Really?' Miss Codell asked, and for the first time, in the faintly rolling 'r' of her

81

'really', Bee heard that she wasn't completely English. It somehow made it easier to answer. She said, 'I'm frightened Thursday's gone off somewhere without telling me. I'm frightened he doesn't know what's happening. He doesn't *know*, Thursday doesn't, about what people are like. I don't want him to get hurt. I don't want him to hurt anyone. I want to be there. Where he is. I could –'

'You could what?'

It sounded daft, but she found she could say it. 'I could, sort of explain. There isn't anyone else, only me.'

Bee was grateful that Miss Codell didn't say any of the things grown-up people, even Bee's Mum, sometimes did, about not thinking you were the only pebble on the beach, or being big headed, or anything like that. She just said, very serious and straight, 'I know. He needs you. If there's any news I'll let you know at once.'

Bee left the school a little happier and grateful. Miss Codell was super, and only a little older than she would be in a few years. But she still wasn't any nearer finding Thursday.

CHAPTER NINE

THE week dawdled by. Bee was stronger, didn't need so much sleep, but because this left longer periods of being awake, she was also bored. She became gloomier as the days passed. The weather was depressing, it was grey, with low clouds, and stickily warm. Bee had a fancy that the air was thick enough to cut with a knife. She wandered round the house aimlessly, not knowing what to do; picked up a pullover she'd started knitting a year before, realized it was now too small for her, and stopped. She went out and did some uninteresting local shopping for her mother. She ate without hunger, sat for hours in front of the television without really looking at the screen, tried to re-read books she'd liked a few years back, but found them childish, she couldn't get involved. Before supper she drifted into the kitchen and leaned against the dresser cupboard, watching her mother rolling pastry on the kitchen table. Four years ago, less, three, or even two, she'd have said 'Can I do that?', and would have made sure there were strips and corners of dough left, after the round pie crust had been cut out, for her to eat raw. Delicious! But today she couldn't be bothered, she didn't want anything in the world as much as the child she had been then had wanted those flabby mouthfuls of uncooked paste.

'If you've nothing to do you could give me a hand,' Mrs Earnshaw said.

'What do you want me to do?'

'Take the chicken meat off the bones and cut it up for me, would you? Then if you've time, there's the carrots to be chopped, and the onion.'

'I hate taking chicken off its bones. I don't know how chickens' bones work. And it's so greasy.'

'Roll out the pastry, then, and I'll do the bird.'

Bee approached the table.

'Wash your hands, girl. I don't care how much you haven't done anything with them all day, you've still to be clean before you touch food.'

Bee rinsed, unwillingly, under the cold tap, and took over the rolling pin. Her mother watched her.

'You'll need more flour under the dough. It'll stick fast if you go on like that.'

Bee sprinkled the marble slab – the remnant of an old washstand – with a teaspoonful of flour and went on rolling. She wasn't interested, she wished she'd stayed upstairs, even though she'd been bored there, and that she hadn't come down so that her mother could order her about. She wouldn't have minded so much if she'd made the pastry from the beginning, then she'd have had a proprietary interest in it, but this helping in someone else's work was just as boring as doing nothing. Worse, because now she was cross as well as bored. She went on passing the rolling pin across the dough without noticing what she was doing, without thinking about it at all.

'Bee! What do you think you're doing? Look at the size of the dough you've rolled it to!'

'You said roll it out,' Bee said.

'Not to the size of the table top. Just for the pie-crust. You know the pie-dish as well as I do. And nice and thick, not a spread of paper like that.'

'I'll do it again,' Bee said. She tried to roll the great sheet of tired dough into a ball, but her mother had been right, it stuck to the marble, and she had to scrape it with a knife, re-flour the slab and start from the beginning. She rolled it out thick, measured the dish, cut out an oval

84

shape, and saw immediately that it was just too small.

'What's the matter?' her mother asked, seeing Bee pick up the rolling pin again.

'It's come out too small.'

'Can't do anything right today, can you?' her mother said.

'It's not my fault.'

'Whose then?'

'All right! Of course it's my fault. Everything's my fault, I suppose. I didn't want to roll the beastly pastry. I don't want to do anything. Nothing's any good, I wish I was dead.'

'If my hands weren't covered with chicken grease I'd give you a slap for that,' Mrs Earnshaw said.

'You wouldn't. I'm much too old to be slapped like a baby!'

'If you're not too old to say wicked, daft things like you wish you were dead, you're not too old to be punished for them.'

'Well, I do. I can't see the point of being alive if everything's going to be so horrible.'

Her mother didn't answer.

'I wish I'd never been born!'

'Leave that pastry alone, then. If you touch it feeling like you do, it'll come out as stiff as a coffin lid.'

Bee threw down the rolling pin. It dented the oval of dough and a cloud of flour flew up.

'You can have your bloody pastry!'

'I won't have you using that language in this house,' Mrs Earnshaw said sharply.

'What's so special about this house? I say bloody at school, why should I pretend I don't say it at home?'

'You'd better go to your room before you say any more.'

'I bloody well will,' Bee said. She banged out of the

kitchen. If she'd had anything else on her feet but her slippers she'd have banged out of the house. She went upstairs, two at a time, and into her own room, where she threw herself on the bed. She was too angry to cry, not quite far enough out of herself to scream. She'd have liked to lie and kick, but she was too old. She hung her face over the side of the bed and chewed the tasselled edge of the coverlet. Her body felt screwed up with rage, and though her eyes were burning and her throat dry with anger, she didn't feel like tears. 'I hate, I hate,' she was saying almost out loud. She grasped the cotton coverlet with her fists as well as with her teeth. She drummed on the pillows with her fists. She felt mad with everything and everybody. Presently pity for herself took over, and she started to cry, large hot tears that hurt; her throat hurt as she sobbed, she talked out loud now. 'I wish I was dead. I hate everybody. I wish I'd never been born. I wish I was dead.' She didn't actually think about making herself heard downstairs, but she didn't try not to be heard. She moaned, she stifled sobs so that the stifling was louder than the sobs she suppressed. At any moment she expected her mother to burst into the room and give her the clip over the ear she'd threatened.

No one came. Bee's groans died down. There were longer and longer pauses between her outbursts. After a time she reluctantly got up off the bed. She felt awful, and when she glanced in her mirror she saw that she looked as awful as she felt. Her eyelids were dark and swollen, her nose was red. Her tears had washed pale pathways, with black edges, down her cheeks. Funny how when you cried it always seemed to leave your face looking dirty, as if what it did to your eyes and nose and throat wasn't bad enough.

Downstairs a door shut firmly. There were steps in the hall and Bee heard her father call out, as he always did, 'Mum? Anyone at home?' As if Bee's Mum wasn't almost always at home when he got back, generally in the kitchen like now, getting supper ready. He knew it too, he didn't wait for an answer, he went into the kitchen straight away. Bee knew he'd be sitting down now in his chair at the end of the table. He'd say, 'Got a cup of tea, Mum?' and spread out his evening paper. He'd read out bits of it, and Mum would say 'Yes', and 'Is that so?' as if she were listening, just as he'd say 'Mmm' and 'You don't say so' to the things she'd tell him about her day. Neither of them really listening to the other, nor expecting to be listened to. Perhaps it'd seem silly to someone outside, as if they didn't care what happened to the other one, but Bee found it comforting. It was ordinary. It was how families ought to be. People could listen too carefully, talk to each other too much, be too anxious to be attentive or fair or even kind. Sometimes you wanted to be taken for granted, to feel inside someone else's life, not a demanding stranger.

The anger had trickled away. Bee felt tired and old, as if she were eighty or ninety years old, like old Mrs Smith. She was also a little frightened. She'd been rude. If her mother told her father he'd tell her off. He wasn't often angry, so when he did get worked up it was that much worse than when Mrs Earnshaw spoke her mind. Bee washed her face and tidied her hair. She went down the stairs slowly, not looking forward to the next ten minutes.

The kitchen was peaceful. Her father was sitting, just as she'd imagined him, with his cup of tea and his paper. Mrs Earnshaw was dishing peas, delicious-looking green peas, with a knob of butter melting succulently in the middle of the pile. The smell of hot chicken pie made even Bee's knotted stomach relax in anticipation. Her father looked up as she came in.

'Evening, love. What's the matter with you? Has she been taken bad again, Mum?'

'Ask her,' Mrs Earnshaw said.

'I'm all right,' Bee said quickly.

'You don't look it, then. Looks bad, doesn't she, Mum?'

'I'm all right, really.'

Mr Earnshaw looked hard, then went back to his paper. He hadn't been told, then, about the row. Bee went over to the cooker, where her mother was standing.

'Can I help?'

'Put this on the table. It's hot, mind! Take the cloth.'

Mrs Earnshaw followed Bee with the pie. It looked all right. Mr Earnshaw, after the first three mouthfuls, said, as he almost always did, 'Melts in the mouth, your pastry, Mum. Makes marriage worth while.'

'By rights this lot should've been a mouthful of clidge,' his wife said.

'Why's that?'

'I lost my temper. It's bad for the dough.'

'You should have called Bee,' Mr Earnshaw said.

'I doubt that'd have helped,' Mrs Earnshaw said.

Bee said nothing. But at the end of the meal, when her father was sitting in the easy chair finishing his paper, and Bee stood next to her mother by the sink, drying the dishes, as they came out of the hot soapy water, she said, 'I'm sorry, Mum.'

'So you should be. As long as you're living in this house you'll keep your language clean, and you'll speak to me and your father properly. As for wishing you'd never been born, I won't have any more of that either. None of us get asked do we want to be born or not, but once we're here, we're here to stay until the right time comes for us to go, and we've to make the best job we can of it, whether we like it or not.'

'You like it, don't you?' Bee asked, astonished.

'Sometimes I do, sometimes I don't.'

'I thought – you're happy mostly, aren't you?' Bee said. It had never occurred to her that her mother wasn't completely contented with life.

'I've been lucky most ways. I'm not complaining,' Mrs Earnshaw said.

'But you're happy, Mum. Aren't you?' Bee insisted.

'No one's happy all the time, unless they're daft. I've had plenty that's made me happy, and plenty on the other side too. That's about what most people's lives are like, I reckon, some bad some good, and it's up to you what you make of it.'

Bee looked out of the corners of her eyes at her mother and thought how extraordinary people were. You saw the outside face they put on for you and thought you knew what it meant, and then suddenly you discovered there was another person behind it, sharing the face and the voice with the person you'd known, like the two little people in a weather house, who came out separately according to the rain or the sun. She knew her mother had had a hard time when she was a child, but she'd always assumed that since she'd been married and had her own house, everything had gone right for her. Bee would have liked to ask more, but she was frightened to. She didn't want, in a way, to know about her mother's troubles, she wanted to be allowed to go on thinking about her own. But she couldn't just leave it there. She said, 'You're glad you married Dad, aren't you? You wanted Trev and me?' As she spoke she had time to wonder what she'd feel if her mother answered that no, she wished she hadn't married, or that she'd never wanted children, having Trevor and Bee had been a mistake.

'Look out! Wet glass is slippery, you don't want to let it fall,' Mrs Earnshaw said.

'I've got it safe.'

'Those six tumblers are the only set I've left of what we got given when we married.'

'Did you have lots of wedding presents, Mum?'

'Not a lot. It was war-time, you couldn't buy much. And money was short too. My Aunt Jessie gave me those glasses. The lady she worked for gave them her when she married. She hadn't ever used them, though. People didn't in those days, they kept things for best. I did, too, for a bit, and then one day I saw them in the cupboard and it came to me that I might just as well have them out and get something out of using them myself as hoard them up for someone else to break after I've gone.'

'Are they valuable, Mum?'

'I don't suppose so. All the same I don't want them broken yet.'

'You didn't answer my question.'

'What was that?'

'Whether you were pleased you'd married and had us.'

'Not much I can do about it now, if I'm not,' Mrs Earnshaw said.

'Go on, Mum. Tell me, really.'

'Your father's the best man I know. Having children – well, it isn't what you expect it'll be, however many of other people's you've had to do with first. If you're asking if I'm sorry I had you, the answer's no, I'm not. That's as long as you behave yourself, of course. I don't want any cheeky monkeys in the house.'

Mrs Earnshaw would never exaggerate her feelings. Bee had to be satisfied with this, but, knowing her mother as well as she did, she realized that she was forgiven.

She went to bed chastened. She was fed up with herself. She'd not only behaved stupidly and childishly today; she realized she'd done nothing all the week, nothing about

Thursday, that is. It was her mother's words about being happy that had made most impression on her. It was an entirely new idea that no one expected to be happy all the time. Somehow Bee, although like everyone else she certainly hadn't been uninterruptedly happy, had assumed that this was what people expected, or at least hoped for. It hadn't occurred to her that the sort of happiness she had had, in bits, unpredictable, never for certain, was about what most people got if they were lucky. She'd thought, if thought is the right word for some very muddled brain processes, that her unhappinesses were by chance; because she was still a child, because Miss Smith had favourites, because Mum didn't understand. She'd believed that when she was quite grown up and could choose what she did and where she lived, and who with, that happiness would be there too. Or perhaps it would be truer to say that she hadn't thought of being unhappy. Of course she knew that some people were; people who had disabled children, people whose husbands were cruel to them, people who were ill, or who lost all their money or went to prison. But not ordinary people like herself and her Mum. She'd even been smug about it, thinking, as she sat in the kitchen downstairs with the rest of them, 'We're a happy family.' Thinking 'Poor Thursday, he doesn't know what it's like to be us.' Now she wondered. She wondered what her Mum thought about, sitting quiet at the table. What sort of things made her unhappy? What did she worry about? What did she dream at nights? What did she expect from the rest of her life? Perhaps she was as fed up as Bee would have been in her place, to think that the most exciting part of her life must be over, now she'd got married and had her children. Mum couldn't be hoping she'd ever get a marvellous job, that she'd make her name at anything; she'd got Dad, and it was nice that she thought he was the best man in the world, but that wasn't exactly exciting. She might have hoped to win a fortune on the pools, if she or Dad had ever done them, but they didn't. In a way Bee sometimes envied her mother who seemed so secure and settled and safe, but in other ways she was sorry for her because the best part of her life was over, all the things Bee still had to look forward to were behind her. And though it seemed ridiculous, this realization that her mother could still feel unhappiness made Bee see for the first time that her mother hoped as well as feared. Things could happen to her too, good things as well as boring or bad things. Bee went to sleep thinking about hope and fear.

CHAPTER TEN

ON the Saturday morning Jean and Trevor arrived before Bee had finished her breakfast. They'd decided the moment had come for them to go to the West End to buy the pram. Trevor was driving the firm's car. He drove it for them all week and had the use of it for himself at week-ends. They'd called in to see if anyone wanted a lift.

'Not me. I've the week's shopping to get in and the cooking,' Mrs Earnshaw said.

'And Dad won't want to. What about you, Bee?'

She wasn't much interested in prams, and trailing round watching other people shop was the most boring thing she knew. On the other hand she hadn't any plans for the day, and it would be good to get out of her bit of London for a change. She felt she hadn't seen anything new for a year.

'Come along. It'd do you good. See some life,' Jean said.

'Is that all you're going to get? Just the pram?'

'We'll have a good look round, too. You don't have to stick with us. Don't you need anything yourself? Shoes? You can't have got all your summer things already?'

'It's just I haven't thought about what I want.' She also wasn't sure how much money she had and didn't want to say so outright in case it looked as if she was asking for more. Dad had a way of pulling out a couple of pound notes on occasions like this and handing them over; Bee had seen her mother's face when this happened and knew she didn't really approve.

'There must be something you want,' Jean said.

Surprisingly, it was Mrs Earnshaw who answered. 'She needs something different to wear after all these weeks.

She's grown a tidy bit too. Get yourself a dress or some-thing. I was going to give you this for your birthday, but you'd better have it now.'

She took something out of the cracked milkjug on the top shelf and put it into Bee's surprised hand.

'Mum! But that's your egg money!'

'That's what egg money's for.'

'What's egg money? You don't keep hens, Trev's Mum,' Jean said.

'Not that kind of egg. Nest egg.'

'I know. My Gran used to call it rainy day money.'

'That's right.'

'Mum! There's five pounds here!'

'Think you won't be able to spend it?'

'Are you sure? All that?'

'You can bring me the change,' Mrs Earnshaw said.

'Super. Marvellous. I'll buy . . . *thanks* Mum. I'll be ready in a second,' Bee called, taking the stairs two at a time, suddenly tinglingly alive at the thought of new clothes. A dress, dark blue, spotted in tiny white pin-pricks, with ruffles at the neck and cuffs, like Janice's. A tight-fitting bright pink ribbed cotton jersey top, with a pale skirt. Sea-green corduroy jeans. A shiny white plastic mac. She couldn't wait to get to the shops.

The shops were choked with customers. It seemed as if everyone else in London had had the same idea that Satur-day morning. Trevor and Jean and Bee pushed their way along the pavements, squeezed themselves into lifts, were jostled through different departments. Jean was marvellous. She never stopped talking and she never lost her temper. Even when a sweating red-faced woman pushed against her with the handle of the pushchair, which by rights shouldn't have been allowed in the lift, all Jean said was, 'Do you mind? Your little boy's chair is sticking into my baby's head.' The woman looked angrily round for the baby, saw Jean's comfortably swelling belly, and said, 'Well!' but didn't get any further. 'By rights you didn't ought to have that chair in this lift,' the liftman said, grumbling, though he hadn't said a word against it before. The woman began to scold the little boy for fidgeting, which he wasn't, and Jean said, in her clear unembarrassed voice, 'Don't worry. It'd take more than a bit of a push with a chair handle to make my baby keep still. He's getting ready for the next Olympics if the antics he's up to now are anything to go on.'

They went first to look for Bee's clothes. Jean insisted. She sent Trevor off to the sports department – 'He's no good on what looks right and what doesn't, and it's a drag having him looking bored all the time you're trying on,' she said. Bee hadn't been sure she wanted Jean with her while she went through the possible dresses, tops, trousers and skirts, making up her mind what she wanted and what she didn't. But Jean turned out to be super here too. Unlike Bee's Mum, she didn't say, 'If you're looking for an after-noon dress, my girl, there's no point in spending an hour sorting through beachwear.' Jean seemed perfectly happy to follow Bee round, looking at everything she wanted to. And if Bee said, 'That's nice,' she didn't immediately – as Mrs Earnshaw would have done – point out that it cost more than Bee had got, or that there wasn't much point in buying a chunky sweater in May. Finally, after terrible difficulties, Bee made up her mind for a silky textured ivory-coloured top and skirt, with a dark brown handkerchief scarf knotted at the throat. 'I couldn't ever carry off that line, even if I wasn't eight months gone, but you can. You just mustn't put on much for the rest of the summer. But that pale colour's wonderful with your hair and eyes,' Jean said, unenvious and happily short, fair and plump. Bee loved Jean. She was glad Trev had found and married her. Jean was super.

'Now for prams,' Jean said. She looked at Bee and laughed. 'You don't want to come, do you? Why don't you go and have a coffee while we're looking? I mean to take ages, I'm warning you.'

'All right. Where'll I meet you, though?'

'In the coffee place, then we can all sit down. I'll need to by then and you look as if you could do with it now.'

Bee realized that Jean was right. Her legs were shaking and her head ached. She was too hot and she felt trembly. 'Which coffee place?' she asked.

'There's one just round the corner, next to the big Sparks and Bangers. Called something like the Treasure Trove, only it isn't that. Something to do with gold, though, or eggs. Anyway you can't miss it, it's right next door to Sparks. You might have a look in there too, if you wanted.'

'What time will you be there?' Bee asked.

'Half an hour? No, that'll mean we have to hurry. Look, it's nearly eleven now. Say twelve. And don't be surprised if we're late, I might think of something else I need. Wait for us, anyway, and we'll wait for you, in case you want to go off and do some more shopping on your own. Got any money? Here – take some. And eat something, do.'

The coffee shop was called the Crock of Gold, and Bee was thankful to sit down and drink a hot sweet liquid which wasn't much like coffee, but wasn't any more like anything else. It did her good, however. Her legs stopped shaking and her head cleared. She ate a bun with sugar on top. It was not fresh, and it contained two currants and one tired sultana. Bee counted. In spite of this, it completed the cure begun by the non-coffee. Twenty minutes after she'd crawled into the shop, Bee felt quite different. She felt strong enough to start off again, and there didn't seem much point in sitting there for another forty minutes, waiting for the others who, she knew, would be late. She still had thirty pence left out of the five pounds. She would go window shopping. She might see exactly the thing she wanted, though at the moment she hadn't any idea what it might be. But that was what window shopping was for, to show you the things you didn't know you needed.

It was hotter than ever out on the pavements, and the crowds had grown. People swarmed in and out of the shop doors in the busy, purposive way ants run in and out of their hills; but trying to get past the dawdlers in the street was, Bee thought, like a fly must feel, trying to walk through a spoonful of jam. There were always people blocking her way, walking in spread-out groups of threes and fours, very slowly in front of her, or stepping sideways just when she thought her passage was clear. Even the shop windows were difficult to get to. The sluggish tide of human bodies meandered in one direction and then in the other, and clumps of solid people prevented her from seeing all she wanted or from moving at all fast. Bee felt herself tiring, and getting cross. She'd better call it a day and get back to the coffee shop. Just as she'd thought this, her eye fell on something in the window she was squashed up against and couldn't get away from. It was a window of china, not one Bee would have chosen to have to spend time with. When she'd first found herself wedged there she'd looked casually at stacks of blue-edged plates, fancy vegetable dishes and twisted teapots. But now, suddenly, she saw that right in the front, down almost on a level with her ankles, there was a row of jugs. Ten of them, different sizes, going from the smallest, barely big enough for cream, right up to a really huge one, large enough to pour cider for a party. They were reddish-brown, unglazed earthenware, with just a little shine round their cream-coloured lips.

They looked out of place in that window of ornamented, elaborate cups and plates and dishes. They marched across the window like uncompromising, earthy peasants, protesting against patterns that didn't mean anything and shapes that were fussy without being useful. Bee loved them at once. She saw immediately that one of them belonged to her mother. It was just the sort of thing Mrs Earnshaw would like, would use every day. They weren't elegant, they weren't for keeping for best, like the glasses, they were everyday jugs. Bee wished she could buy the lot.

It turned out that she could only get one. They were French, she discovered, and her thirty pence was only four pence more than she needed for the smallest but one. She came out of the shop carrying it carefully, filled with the happy knowledge that she'd got exactly the right present for the right person. It would be perfect to have something to take back to Mum for herself. A sort of thank you for the morning's success. Bee thought of how she'd looked in the ivory suit. That had felt right too. In spite of being tired, Bee glowed.

She started back toward the Crock of Gold. There was no hurry. Jean wouldn't be there for another ten minutes at least, and then she'd want to sit and recover for a bit. Bee drifted with the crowd. She stopped to listen to a man on the pavement calling his wares; ropes of artificial pearls, tinted different colours. Bee could just hear how her mother would sniff at that sort of thing. She didn't want pearls herself, not at all, but she didn't think they looked too bad as the man held them up in the sunlight. Next she hesitated by a shoe shop. Marvellous shoes, she desperately wanted a pair of cream-coloured buckle shoes which would have looked super with her new suit. But she had four pence left from the five pounds, so it was no good longing. She dropped the four pence into the shabby violin case of a man who was standing on the edge of the pavement, playing a piece Bee knew but couldn't put a name to. He didn't thank her. Perhaps four pence hardly counted. Bee felt satisfied that she'd got rid of it, though. It was tidy to have spent the whole lot almost at one go.

There was a knot of people in front of her, looking through a sort of peephole in the hoardings which bordered this bit of the street. A new building was going up there. A gigantic crane pushed its head up, like a giraffe's, into the sky overhead. Bee could hear the sound of electric drills above the noise of the traffic. She waited her turn to step up to the little platform on to which the window gave. She enjoyed watching other people work.

When she got there and looked down, she couldn't at first see anything. The site wasn't ready yet to be built on, it was still in the process of being cleared. There was a haze of yellow dust over it, which made it all look unreal. The figures of the men engaged in the demolition work were indistinct, Bee could only just see that they were drilling at concrete foundations, hacking at the remains of walls. The great crane wasn't in use yet, it hung over the site like a watchful animal waiting its turn. Most of the walls were down, but at one side there was a step or two of a staircase. Two men were prising chunks of it away with picks. Bee wondered how long it would take, if everything stopped now, if no one did any more work on this site for ages, before it came to look like her own empty site. How long would it take for earth to come sifting back over the concrete, for seeds to fall and take root, for grass and weeds and saplings to spring up and for this dusty, city-centred place to go wild? No one would ever have guessed when the bomb fell that her site would become a place where bees gorged themselves in buddleia flowers and hawk moths laid their eggs, right in the middle of London, with the traffic screeching outside and the railway line running overhead.

Someone blew a whistle and there was a change on the site. The electric drill stopped. The two men with picks slowed down and stood looking at what they'd done. A figure came out of a sort of shed at one side and shouted. The whistle blew again. The men began walking across the site towards the shed. They were packing up for the day.

Bee, looking at them idly, still wondering about what she thought of as 'the jungle taking over', wasn't really looking at any one of them, but without knowing she was doing it, she counted them. Two had been drilling. They were stacking the drills in the cradle of the crane. One had come up out of some deeper cellar. He disappeared into the shed. The two who had been destroying the staircase had got rid of their picks and were coming off the site. They weren't walking together, the front one walked quickly as if he were trying to get rid of the other, who was stumbling after him. The one behind was short and stout, he looked as if he had difficulty in keeping up. But the front one didn't turn round, he looked aloof, lonely. Bee looked away from him, then back again. He was too far away for her to be able to see his face, you couldn't possibly find an unknown workman on a building site interesting or attractive from a distance of two hundred yards. She didn't know why she continued to stare after his retreating back. He was up at the top of the ramp that led down from the level of the road on the further side of the site, now, and had perhaps another twenty yards to go before reaching the exit door in the hoarding, still walking fast and without turning round. He was slight, about average height, young. At this moment two things happened. He took off the flat cap that he, and all the other men, wore and shook his longish thick dark hair; and he hesitated for a fraction in his quick tread. One of his feet dragged, didn't absolutely clear the ground.

Bee put her hands on the edge of the window into the site and called to him. But she knew it was no use, he couldn't have heard her, if her voice had been twice as loud, above the roar of the traffic and the voices of the crowd behind her. But for a moment she almost thought he had, for he hesitated again and looked for the first time in her direction, and now she saw the streak of hair that always fell across his forehead and she thought she could distinguish his dark eyebrows tilted up at the outer corners. She waved, desperately crying out his name, 'Thursday!' He gave no sign of having seen her or heard her. He turned his back on her and went through the doorway into the street beyond.

Bee backed. She said to a woman standing behind her, 'Where does that door lead to?' The woman stared.

'The other side of the building site? Where is it?'

'I've no idea, I'm sure,' the woman said, moving away hurriedly. She obviously thought Bee was crazy.

'Over there. Where does it come out into?' Bee asked a man who had been standing next to her at the window.

'One of the streets the other side. Parallel with Oxford Street it must be,' someone said.

'How can I get there?' Bee asked urgently.

'Down Newman Street.' 'It'll be Poland Street, more likely.' 'Quickest way is to cut through the passage.' There were as many opinions as voices. Bee didn't wait. She ran.

It would be truer to say she tried to run. But if getting through the crowds before, when she hadn't been in a hurry, was like a fly walking through jam, this journey was more like those nightmare flights when you are desperate to reach somewhere, or to get away from something, and every step is weighted and slow. It seemed now as if the people deliberately formed themselves into knots and clusters in front of her. She pushed, she shoved, at last she fought. She heard objections, protests, she didn't care, she had to get through. She reached the side-turning, relatively empty of people, and she ran. She came to a cross-roads and saw, to her left, the hoarding at the back of the building site, the doorway, workmen coming out in twos and threes, some coming towards her, some going the other way.

It would have been too much to hope for that Thursday might have been coming her way. The men she passed were all much older, dustier, tireder than Thursday could have been. She ran past them and beyond the doorway. If he hadn't come out in her direction, he must have gone in the other. The narrow little street ended in a T-junction; on the right was a long, slightly wider street, one-way, with cars pushing to get up it, the pavements alive with pedestrians. If you turned left you would come to Oxford Street, which Bee had just left. She looked in both directions. It was hopeless. There were too many people, she couldn't have found Thursday among them even if she'd known which direction he'd taken. He might as well have been immediately swallowed in those crowds she'd fought through. There wasn't the smallest chance of finding him.

If she had stood still she would have let out the tears that burned behind her eyes. Anger saved her. She'd been so near, she couldn't give up now. She went back to the door in the hoarding. She didn't dare to give herself time to think, or she wouldn't have the courage to act. She stopped the first man coming out and passing her.

'Please.'

'What's wrong, then?' the man asked. He wasn't unfriendly, but he wasn't interested and he was in a hurry. He kept on walking, Bee had to half run to keep up with him.

'I'm looking for a friend. I saw him just now down there and then he went out of that door and I couldn't get there in time to catch up with him.'

'Too bad,' the man said, but he walked a little slower.

'He's called Townsend.'

'Come again?' the man said.

'He's called Townsend.'

'Tall chap? With glasses?'

'Not specially tall. And he doesn't wear glasses.'

'Why don't you come and have a cup of coffee and tell me all about it?' the man said.

'I don't want any coffee. Thank you. I just want to find Thursday.'

'Come on, now. Aren't I as good as him any day of the week? It's a shame if he keeps a pretty girl like you waiting around for him,' the man said. He put a hand under her elbow as if to guide her.

So this was what happened. This was a pick-up, what the girls at school talked about, half-knowledgeable, half-frightened. This was what happened if you did as your mother had always told you not to, and talked to strange men. Bee said 'No,' and took a step backwards. She looked up and down the little street. It wasn't deserted, but no one was very near. It seemed that there weren't any more workmen coming off the building site. Bee was frightened, but she also felt collected. She said, 'Thank you very much. If you don't know anything about Thursday I'll ask some-one else.'

'Why trouble yourself about him when you've got me ready and willing to treat you to a cup of whatever you'd fancy?' the man said.

'I've got to find him. He's been gone for weeks. The police are looking for him,' Bee said.

'What's that with the police?' the man said, dropping his hand from Bee's elbow immediately.

'They're looking for him. That's why I must . . .'

'Maybe the foreman might know something. Why don't you ask him? He's down there yet,' the man said, nodding towards the doorway on to the site. Bee's eyes followed his down towards the dusty, broken ground below them. When she looked back, the man was already halfway along the street. The mention of the police had scared him, he didn't want to get mixed up in anything. In spite of being glad he'd gone, Bee felt stupidly lonely and helpless. She felt as if she'd used up all her courage in asking this man, who'd been worse than useless, about Thursday. She didn't want to have to go to talk to another.

But there wasn't any choice. She had seen Thursday. The foreman might be able to tell her something that would help her to find him.

The ramp was covered with yellow dust. Her shoes left white marks all the way down. It was quieter down here, too, and she was conscious of the sound of her steps, and of hundreds of eyes gazing at her from the little window up above where she'd been standing a short time ago. She could imagine what the voices that went with those eyes would be saying. 'Look! A girl! Wonder what she's doing, down there? After one of the men, most likely. What, a young girl like that? Girls nowadays aren't like they used to be. Running after boys all the time, that's what they do. Look! A bird! Whose bird? Ask me another. Anyone's bird, if you ask me. Looking for trouble.' A long wolf whistle sounded from the window opening on Oxford Street. Bee thought of her mother and her knees trembled. 'Making a show of yourself,' would have been the mildest thing Mrs Earnshaw might have said. It wasn't that it was in any way dangerous. What could happen to her, to Bee, here, under the scrutiny of a thousand distant, incurious eyes? It was what it looked like that was awful. Bee could see herself, from a thousand miles off, walking alone on to a building site full of men, as if she'd been a Night Club queen demanding attention, or a fashion model parading to be ogled. And she didn't feel like either of these. She felt like what she was, a gawky schoolgirl in the most ordinary clothes, who had never learned how to walk or how to hold herself or how not to blush scarlet all down her neck when boys cat-called or men whistled at her.

The site was a huge empty mess. The ground was uneven, there were steps up and down, huge humps here and there, half a basement exposed below her feet, the giant crane hovering overhead. It was almost silent down here, compared with the hurly-burly up above. Bee thought suddenly – why? – of a quotation, from some play, she couldn't remember what. 'Will you walk out of the air, my lord?' 'Into my grave.' Into my grave. Oh God, Thursday! Into my grave.

Hoisting herself back to sanity, she found the hut which still had its door open, and looked inside. This must be the foreman, sitting on a high stool against an even higher desk, running his finger down a column in a book. Bee said, 'Please!'

The man turned and looked at her with astonishment.

'No one isn't allowed on this site except it's on business,' he said.

'I only want to ask you one thing. About someone working here – he's called Townsend.'

'Never heard of him,' the man said at once.

'He was here this morning. I saw him going out of that door up there.'

'If you saw him, what're you asking me about, then?' the man said.

'He'd gone by the time I got round there,' Bee said.

'What d'you think I can tell you about him? We don't keep lists of their home addresses, you know,' the man said.

'But you'd have his name somewhere?' Bee said. She didn't know how she managed to be so persistent, except that she was desperate.

'If you saw him, what good'll that do you?'

'I think it was him. I just want to be sure. He was a long way away.'

'What's the name, then?'

'Townsend.'

The foreman looked down a sheet of names. 'Nothing like that here.'

'There must be!' Bee said.

'I told you, it's not here.'

'He might be using a different name. If I told you what he's like you might know him. He's fairly tall, he's not very old, he's got this thick hair, black, and it sort of falls over one eye all the time.'

'What do you think we are? Bleeding enquiry agents? I've never set eyes on him as far as I know. If you saw him, then he was there. Now run away. I've got to shut up and get home for my dinner.'

It was horrible walking back across the deserted site. Without looking up Bee could feel the eyes gimleting into her back, the thoughts going through the heads of those unknown, casual shoppers up there at the Oxford Street window. She was also fighting the lump in her throat, the terrible need to cry, which she wouldn't give way to here with the busy, unsympathetic foreman just behind her and all those faces peering down. She reached the door leading off the site, remembered Jean and Trevor, and half ran, fighting her way again through the crowds, thicker than ever, to the Crock of Gold. Jean and Trev were sitting there peacefully, drinking tea. Bee joined them, but at the first word they spoke to her, her self-control gave way, and she cried hot, ashamed tears.

CHAPTER ELEVEN

'HE'S alive! He's not in hospital dangerously ill. He's not lying somewhere dead and undiscovered. Thursday's alive,' was what rang through Bee's mind for the rest of the week-end. But it couldn't make her happy, there was still too much she didn't know. And waking very early on Sunday morning, when the sky was just beginning to get light over the roofs of the houses opposite, and the birds were trying their voices out in emphatic, repetitive twitterings, she went over yesterday's scene again, and her heart lurched as she remembered that the boy she had seen had been so far off, needn't have been Thursday at all. There could be other young men of his height, with his dark hair. And his walk? That characteristic hesitation? Now she saw that there might be a hundred boys who walked like that. It could have been a stumbling on the uneven ground. At four o'clock in the morning, all the reasons why it might not have been Thursday crowded in on her. What was he doing this week-end alone? It was three weeks since he'd gone. Had he been quite by himself all that time? He wasn't a great talker, didn't look for company as much as most boys of his age, but could he really want to be alone for so long? Why had he given a false name? And then the worst sus-picions came back. Had he done something terrible and had to hide? Perhaps the police were after him for a crime, not just because he was missing? Perhaps – and this was the worst thought of all – she had only imagined she'd seen him, and really he was unconscious somewhere, or dead. Bee's mind raced. She didn't know how to lie still. She wanted to be up and looking. She knew she must go back to the building site, on Monday, and she didn't want to go. She lay awake for hours, her mind going over and over the same facts and ideas in the way that your fingers worry a knotted string, getting tired and bruised, but not getting any further towards the untying of it. At last she dozed, then slept deeply and didn't wake till late on the Sunday morning.

The kitchen was full of bright sunshine when she came down. Her mother was preparing the dinner, and Lynne was sitting at the table drinking tea.

'Here she is. I told you she wouldn't be long.'

'Hi, lazybones! I wish my Mum'd let me sleep till eleven, Sundays.'

'Get yourself a cup, Bee. There's plenty in the pot. Toast?'

'No, thanks.'

'Boiled egg? You can cook yourself some bacon if you like.'

'Just tea. I'm not hungry.'

'You should eat something. You hardly touched your supper, yesterday,' Mrs Earnshaw said.

'I'll eat lunch,' Bee said.

'You want to eat when you've not been well. You don't look right yet. Have you heard anything from Thursday, Bee?' Lynne asked.

'Give her time to have a cup of tea, Lynne,' Mrs Earnshaw said.

'I'm sorry. I'm always putting my great foot in it. Only I really wanted to know.'

'It's all right,' Bee said. It wasn't, she could hardly make herself say his name without the quick tears pricking behind her eyelids, but at the same time she was glad Lynne did want to know. It made him seem less far away, at least remembered, not pushed out of sight and out of mind as if he'd been dead.

'You haven't heard from him, then?'

'No.'

'You look so worried. Do stop worrying. He'll be all right,' Lynne said, in her comforting, friendly voice.

'What makes you say that, Lynne?' Bee's mother asked.

'I dunno. You know, Mrs Earnshaw, there are some people, however hard they try they're always going to turn out unlucky. Like Margie Banks, Bee, at school. Whenever there's trouble she's always in it. Even when it's nothing to do with her really, she always manages to turn up just when there's a bust-up, and then everyone thinks she's been in on it from the start. Or take when she started going around with Johnny Mellish. Only a month after she'd been going with him he was put on probation for nicking tins out of the supermarket. And as if that wasn't enough, she went out next with that coloured boy, Michael Christian, and the first night their tube train broke down and she didn't get home till three o'clock in the morning. Her father walloped her. She told me. And it really wasn't her fault, they hadn't done anything, just sat in the train with a lot of other people. But that's the sort of thing that always happens to Marge.'

'I know. My Aunt Edie was like that. If there was a stone left in the cherry pie, she'd be the one to break her tooth on it,' Mrs Earnshaw said.

'That's it, exactly. That's Margie.'

'But you mean, Thursday isn't?' Mrs Earnshaw said.

'No, he's not. He's peculiar, I'm not saying he isn't. He makes you feel sometimes like he doesn't want to know you. But he's not dead unlucky, like Margie. He's got – I don't know what it is. Something.'

'Common sense?' Bee's mother suggested.

'Well, it's something like that, but that's not quite right. I can't explain. It's just a sort of feel. You know. You feel someone might do something crazy or wild or just plain silly, but they'd get themselves right again somehow. Not like poor old Margie. She'd always go on doing whatever it was because she wouldn't see what was wrong till it's too late.'

'Is she still going out with Michael?' Bee asked, for something to say.

'Well, she is, only her parents don't know. He waits round the corner for her in the evenings and they go off to the West End somewhere, so's none of the kids round here see them and tell on her.'

'How do you know *I* won't?' Mrs Earnshaw asked, shelling peas very quickly and neatly into a pudding basin.

'You wouldn't!'

'Maybe I won't, and maybe I will. How do you know?' Mrs Earnshaw repeated.

'You're not the kind. You're like my Mum. Least said, soonest mended's what she says. She knows about Margie, but she'd never tell Mrs Banks. Like she says, if anyone came telling her about me, she'd be mad at first and only grateful after. Not that there's much she doesn't know, anyway.'

'What'd you do if someone came and told you something about me?' Bee asked her mother.

'Get her to say it in front of you and hear what you had to say.'

'Suppose I was Margie? I mean, suppose I was meeting a coloured boy and you didn't know.'

'If you were being double-faced about it I'd think something was wrong with you. Or with him,' Mrs Earnshaw said.

'But him being coloured. Would you mind that?'

'Yes, I would.'

'Mum! You're not colour prejudiced!' Bee said, horrified.

'Don't be soft, Bee. I'm not saying I want black people to be treated any different from the whites because they're black. I think they should have their education and their chances same as the rest of us. But if you ask me if I want you marrying one, no, I don't. Just like if you asked me should you marry a Chinaman or a Frenchman or an American, I'd say no. Or a layabout do-nothing, or a lord. I'm not saying it mightn't work, but if you start marrying out of your own kind, you're taking on trouble, that's what I think.'

'But that's awful! You are prejudiced! About all sorts of things.'

'You expect to have picked up some prejudices by the time you're my age,' Mrs Earnshaw agreed.

'Don't you mind being prejudiced though? I don't see how you can just know you are and not do anything about it.'

'Prejudices are like habits. You may wish you hadn't got them, but they do make life simpler. Anyway if you've only just discovered mine they can't be that terrible.'

'You do go on about it, Bee,' Lynne said.

'I don't see how people can be colour prejudiced now,' Bee said.

'You may not see how, but if you don't see they are you've fewer wits than I gave you credit for. And if you married a coloured chap, you'd come in for the thick end of the stick as well as him, and so would your children. If that isn't a reason for not wanting you to marry one of them, I don't know what is,' her mother said.

'What would you say if I wanted to marry a Catholic? Or a Jewish boy?'

'Same as I'd say about the others. If their religion meant a lot to them, that is. As soon as you start with two different ways of thinking, you're asking for more trouble than marrying makes anyway.'

'But you aren't thinking of him as a person! You're saying he must be wrong just because he's got a different religion to us. Or a different coloured skin!'

'Use your loaf, Bee. You didn't say, How would I like you to marry Tom Smith, you just said a coloured chap, or a Mohammedan or such-like. All I know about him, then, is that he's coloured. That's all I'm talking about.'

'My Mum would create if he wasn't English, whoever he was. But then, so would I,' Lynne said comfortably.

'What else would you mind? Suppose I got pregnant without being married?' Bee said.

'Depends on how and why. I don't hold with bringing a child into the world without having a proper home for it,' her mother said.

'Suppose I had an affair with someone without getting pregnant?'

'Thinking of it?' Mrs Earnshaw asked, looking at Bee hard.

'I just wondered.'

'By and large I'm against it. I don't say there mightn't be reasons sometimes why it's the right thing to do, but just like that, plain and simple, I'd not like it. No.'

'Suppose I didn't come back till three in the morning, like Margie? Or stayed out all night?' Bee suggested.

'You'd better have a good reason to give when you do come home, that's all,' her mother said.

'I wish my Mum thought like you. When she started telling me about sex and that, when I was thirteen, she said if ever she caught me sleeping around like some girls do —

you know – she'd tan the hide off me. She says, wait till you've found the right chap and then marry him,' Lynne said.

'Seems I'm not the only one with prejudices, if that's what you call them. More like sense, I'd say,' Mrs Earnshaw said.

'It's all right for me, I'm not very highly sexed, so it doesn't worry me. I like holding Nick's hand, and him hugging me, and dancing and that, but I don't get all worked up the way some girls do,' Lynne said. She poured herself out another cup of tea and helped herself to two generous spoonfuls of sugar. What an extraordinary conversation! Bee thought. Love-making and sex weren't subjects she and her mother discussed much. Practically never, in fact. And here was Lynne talking about them in a perfectly ordinary tone of voice as if she were speaking of the weather. And saying how she herself felt about it too. It was probably just because Lynne was so much at ease that Bee found it possible to talk to her mother like this. She looked at Lynne, and wished she could be like her, in some ways anyhow. Lynne took life calmly and appeared to enjoy it. She was a peaceful person to be with. 'She'll make a marvellous mother,' Bee thought.

'You aren't drinking your tea, Bee,' her mother said.

'When'll you be back at school, Bee? After the exams we're going to put on a play. Alison's sort of in charge and Stella's doing the casting now, so we want to know who'll be there. That's what I really came round to see you about, only I got talking about things, like I always do, and I forgot.'

'I'm no good at acting,' Bee said quickly.

'No, I know. But you do say poetry well, which is more than you can say for most of the others.'

'What's poetry got to do with it?'

'Didn't I tell you? Guess what! What we're supposed to be doing for the play, I mean.'

'*Macbeth*,' Bee said, wondering if she could possibly do the sleepwalking scene.

'*A Midsummer Night's Dream*.'

'We can't! That's what the lower third do, their first year!'

'I know. That's what we all said. But you know what Alison's like.'

'But why does she want to? What's the point? It isn't as if everyone doesn't know it already. We're all of us dead sick of it.'

'Alison sees herself as a great comic actor. Actress, I mean. And Stella does anything Alison says, so we're landed with it.'

'I shan't be in it.'

'You'll have to be. We've all got to, otherwise there aren't enough people to be courtiers and fairies and things. I think you're supposed to be Hermia because you're dark.'

'Hermia was small. Smaller than Helena, anyway. Who's being Helena?'

'Don't know. Claire's going to be Titania, of course.'

'What are you, Lynne?'

'I thought I'd say I wanted to be a fairy, and just see their faces. Can't you imagine me, with a pair of little wings, jumping around, and singing about swinging in a cowslip bell, or whatever it is? I bet I'd be funnier than Alison.'

'Wrong play. That's Ariel. *The Tempest*.'

'I'm sure someone calls them dainty elves. It'd really bring the house down if someone called me that.'

'I think it's awful. I don't know how even Alison could,' Bee said.

'Lots of people don't seem to mind. I must go. I really

only came out to get *Sweet Seventeen* and the Sunday papers for Mum, and then as I had to pass your door I thought I'd just pop in and see how you were getting on. You're better, aren't you, Bee? You look better. When'll you be back at school? You didn't say.'

'Another fortnight. Only I can't possibly do the exams.'

'You'll be let off, I'm sure. Lucky you.'

Bee didn't feel lucky.

'Come with me as far as the paper shop, Bee. I'm sure you want papers or a book or something.'

'I'll come with you, but I won't come in.' She didn't want to see old Mrs Smith again. She was angry again when she remembered their last conversation. They walked out on to the hot sunny pavements, Lynne chattering, Bee hardly attending at all. She waited outside Cooper's while Lynne spent what seemed an unnecessarily long time choosing her papers. She hoped neither of the old couple would come out and see her standing there, clear of the doorway. When at last Lynne emerged, Bee hurried her away.

'What's the hurry? You feeling bad?' Lynne asked.

'It's just I didn't want to talk to any of them in there.'

'She's all right. The old lady. I like the way she talks. She's ever so fond of Thursday, too. She was going on and on about him today.'

'What did she say?'

'I couldn't understand it all. She uses funny words. Sounded as if she thought he'd got stuck somewhere and couldn't get home. 'Least that's what I think she was saying.'

'Anything else?'

'Not really. Oh, I know. She said only one person'd be able to get him back.'

'Who?'

'I thought she meant it'd be you.'

'Did she say me?'

'Not exactly. But it must've been you.'

'How do you know? What did she say?'

'I told you, I'm not sure what she meant. Something about it'd be the person who liked him, or that he likes, or something.' Bee was astonished to see that Lynne, the easy Lynne, was embarrassed.

'I must get back. 'Bye, Bee. See you,' Lynne said in a hurry, and walked off. Bee went slowly home, pondering what she'd heard. She was half angry, half mollified. Old Mrs Smith had no right even to wonder what she and Thursday felt about each other. On the other hand it was comforting to have it taken for granted that there was something special between them. And Mrs Smith's saying that she, Bee, would be the person to help him was what she believed herself. She wondered just how the old lady had put it so that Lynne found it embarrassing to repeat. She wondered all the way home.

On Monday she went back to Oxford Street.

CHAPTER TWELVE

SHE timed herself to reach the site before the lunch break. She supposed this would be about midday. At a quarter to twelve she was at the observation window, looking down again at the steam drills and the cranes and the girders and the cement mixers and at the men around them. The men were almost as indistinguishable as the machines. There were some who couldn't possibly be Thursday, but there were also several who might be. She'd have to wait till she could see him near.

At five to twelve she walked round the site to the exit in the back street. She hoped there weren't any other ways out. She stood on the opposite side of the road, trying to look as if she was interested in a greengrocer's shop. A minute after she'd got there, she heard the siren go for the midday break. Seconds later men began to come out of the opening to the site. She hadn't arrived a moment too early.

They came out in twos and threes. Bee didn't have to look directly at them. Out of the corner of her eye, with a fraction of her hearing, she would know him. She discovered too, that the plate glass in front of the hideously expensive strawberries and the polished apples reflected the street almost as well as a mirror. While standing with her back to the doorway she could see everyone coming out.

Thursday wasn't one of the first. The stream of men had slackened to a trickle before he appeared. He came out by himself, looked round, and turned right, the opposite direction to that taken by most of the others. Bee was grateful for that; it meant she wouldn't be confronting him before his fellow workers. She followed him, giving him time to get right away from the site. If he wanted to throw off his colleagues, so did she. He turned left, then right. He didn't look round. Bee could follow him in safety. She turned the corner twenty yards behind him and was in a little mews, sloping down to a lower level than the roads they'd just left. It was like a doll's world, tiny houses with brightly painted doors and window boxes, and bright flowers, pink and royal blue. There were one or two cars parked, but they were on a different scale, enormous, black, glossy. But there were no other people. Perhaps it was this emptiness as well as the sudden change of sizes compared with the streets outside, which made Bee feel as if it wasn't quite real. It was also very quiet.

She called his name. 'Thursday!'

He didn't turn.

Bee called again, louder. 'Thursday! Wait!'

She wasn't sure whether he'd hesitated, but he didn't turn, didn't stop. The point he'd reached was where the cobbled mews road began to rise, preparatory to joining the next street. Knowing she must catch him up before he got there, Bee began to run.

At the sound of her footsteps, he did look round, but only for a moment, then turned away and continued to walk. Bee doubled her speed and reached him just before a great stone arch led back to the ordinary world, by the prettiest miniature house of them all, gay with yellow paint and scarlet flowers, but somehow heartless, every window shut, every ruffled muslin curtain secretively correct. Bee touched Thursday's arm and was frightened herself by his recoil.

'It's all right, Thursday. It's only me.'

He looked at her with blank eyes.

'Thursday, it's me, Bee.'

He shook his head, not as a negative, but as if to clear it.

Bee, looking at him with love and fear, saw that he was thinner, paler, and that he was wearing what she thought of as his shut-in look, the expression that meant he couldn't listen properly to what was being said to him, couldn't respond to warmth, couldn't let himself feel. Bee knew what that meant. It went with unhappiness. Molly's treatment had brought it before now, he'd had it when his father had been put away, sometimes it had appeared to have no cause, it just happened. Bee had learned to dread it. She'd also learned that when she saw it she must leave Thursday alone. But this was too desperate a situation, she had to try to get through.

'Thursday, please. Please listen. I must ask you what's been happening. Why did you go like that? What have you been doing? Where have you been?'

He moved a step back from her and stood, still looking at her, but without any movement which might show that he heard her.

'Please, Thursday. You could tell me. If it's a secret I won't tell, you know I won't. I'm safe. I'd never give you away.'

He shook his head again, but again it wasn't in answer to her words as much as to some inner colloquy.

'What is it? What's the matter? Won't you speak to me?' Bee cried. She wondered for a moment if she could have been mistaken as Lynne had been, if there really was another boy looking like Thursday but not he. But her hungry eyes told her that this was the same one, about whom she knew so much, whom she'd seen in so many different moods that even this one of estrangement and silence was part of a familiar person.

'Thursday, it's Bee. Have you forgotten?'

His lips moved as if he were trying the name 'Bee', but no sound came.

'Perhaps you've forgotten everything?'

His eyes travelled over her as if he were looking for some landmark which might recall to his mind a once known country, but he still didn't speak.

'If you've lost your memory you might not remember anything. I know you didn't give your real name where you're working. Is that what it is? Do you know who you are? Do you remember me? We're at school together, the Pottery Lane school. Your name is Thursday, you live in Springhurst Terrace. The name of the mistress who takes our form is Miss Stevens. You do remember, don't you? Thursday? You do remember me?'

But he still stood, just looking. Bee stepped forward and put her hand on his arm. He cried out, 'Don't touch me,' and leapt back as if she had stung him.

Bee said, 'Thursday!'

'Go away.'

'You do know who I am? You haven't forgotten everything?'

'I haven't forgotten.'

'What's the matter, then? Why don't you want me?'

'I don't want anyone. I just want to be left alone.'

'I know. I won't bother you, truly I won't. But it's so long since I've seen you, and no one knows where you are, and I thought something awful must have happened.'

'Nothing's happened. I wanted to be alone, that's all.'

'You could have told me you were going.'

'You'd have tried to get hold of me. I told you, I had to get away.'

'Why? What's wrong?'

'I'm perfectly all right,' Thursday said, in the flat voice, with no change of expression, that was so anything but all right.

'Where are you living, then?'

No answer.

'When will you come back?'

'I don't know if I shall come back.'

'Never?' Bee asked, feeling tightened like the string on a violin, ready to break at any moment.

'I shouldn't think so. There's nothing to come back for.'

'Not for me?' She hadn't meant to say it, it came out quickly before she could harden her lips to keep it in.

He said, 'No.' His indifference was worse than anger.

'Don't go. Wait a minute. Even if you don't want me, there's something you ought to know. The police are looking for you. Because you're missing.'

He was as quiet about this as about everything else. 'Who put them on to me? Was it you?'

'Of course it wasn't.' She hesitated before telling him about Mr Tenterden, and before she'd spoken again, he said, 'I know who it was.'

'Who?'

'I know. They're against me.' But he always spoke with that sense of not caring, as if he knew everything but was beyond being hurt, beyond minding, beyond human feeling, beyond love.

'Who's against you? Is it something to do with Molly?'

'She's probably in it too.'

'Who else? Who's against you? Tell me, perhaps I could help.'

'No one can help.'

'I'd try. You know I'm not against you, don't you?'

'Aren't you?' But it wasn't a question, more of a comment, as if she'd said, 'It's a miserable day' and he'd said, 'Isn't it?'

'Who are they who're against you? Who's doing something against you? Please tell me.'

'You wouldn't understand.'

'I might. Try.'

'It's too complicated. I can't explain.'

'You don't want to.'

'No.'

'Isn't there anything I can do to help?'

'No. Thank you. Only go away.'

His politeness was horrible. Bee felt like shouting, saying something outrageous, doing something which would break his cold mask, which would get a reaction, even a hostile one.

'What are you going to do?'

'That's nothing to do with you,' he said, not unkindly, as if he were stating a known fact.

'It is. Please tell me.'

'I don't know. I never know what's going to happen. They decide.'

'But who are they?'

'Sometimes it's one person, sometimes another. I can never be sure.'

'Why should they stop you seeing me?'

'They don't. You're here, aren't you?'

'Don't you want to see me again?'

He said, 'No,' in the flat voice that made Bee believe she couldn't have heard what he said, because you couldn't say words like that, dreadful, hurting words, in a tone without spite or anger or feeling of any kind. It was like hearing a machine talking, like hearing a computer swear, all the meaning taken out of the bad words by the deadness of the intonation, so that you listened again to the syllables that had just been propelled into the air, to make sure they were what you seemed to have heard, but which should have had human feeling and meaning behind them.

'You shouldn't cry. You look ugly when you cry,' he said. He turned away, towards the great stone arch. Bee started after him, too desperate to think of anything but not letting him go. He looked round and said, in the same sleep-walking tones, 'Go back. I just want to be left alone.'

She stood still, then, her eyes shut to try to prevent the tears from running down her cheeks. She heard his footsteps receding, one, two, one, two, one, two, one – where there should have been the hesitation, there was a halt. A voice called.

'Bee!'

She had a rush of hope, turned her opened eyes towards him, and through the distorting waters of her tears, saw his figure wavering at the gate.

'If they ask, say no one need bother, I'm all right on my own.'

Bee cried, 'Let me come too!' It came out hoarse like the cry of a hurt animal, the words choked and indistinct. If Thursday had heard them, he took no notice. He walked on, through the archway, round the corner, out of sight. Bee didn't follow. She stood in the sunny mews, surrounded by heartless glossy paint and prim cultivated plants, which had nothing to do with misery and loss and pain.

CHAPTER THIRTEEN

HER mother took one look at her when she got back, then took her into the kitchen and sat her on a chair. When she'd put on the kettle, she came and sat next to Bee, close, and said, 'Let up, lass. It's best all out.'

Bee sobbed. She started by just letting the tears roll down her cheeks, but as she re-lived in her mind the happenings of that horrible morning, tears weren't enough. It took the deep sobs that hurt her throat and jolted her whole body to express her anger as well as her grief. She was anxious and unhappy, but she was also hurt and furious. She heard Thursday's voice in her inside ear, saying in that cold, un-convincing tone, 'Only go away.' 'No,' to the question didn't he want to see her. 'You look ugly when you cry.' For that she cried more than ever, as if by making herself ugly she could punish him.

'Your tea. And you've to stop crying. Whatever's gone wrong, I reckon you've got it out of your system by now,' Mrs Earnshaw said, putting the cup down beside her.

Bee drank the tea. It was scalding hot and very sweet. Surprisingly, it made it easier to stop crying. After two cups she could look at her mother without more than the occasional shiver which is the aftermath of an outburst of crying. She felt exhausted but a little relieved.

'Want to tell me?' her mother said.

Bee shook her head. Then nodded it.

'Make up your mind.'

'I don't know.'

'I can wait.' It was unusual for Mrs Earnshaw to sit still

with nothing in her hands. It made the occasion more important.

'You've seen the lad,' Mrs Earnshaw said, statement not question.

'Mm.'

'You've been up West to see him. You saw him Saturday when you were with Trev and Jean, and you've been back to look for him again.'

'How did you guess?' Bee asked, surprised.

'Look about you when you came back last time, I reckon. You can't always say why you know things, you just know them. Another cup?' her mother said.

'Yes, please.'

While she was drinking it, her mother said abruptly, 'How is he?'

Bee shook her head.

'He isn't sick?'

'He's terribly thin.'

'He's never been a Harry at the best of times. That all that's wrong with him?'

'He's different.'

'What d'you mean, different?'

'He talks differently.'

'But he wasn't talking wild? Silly stuff?'

'You mean as if he was mad? Thursday's not mad!' Bee cried out.

'He's had enough to turn anyone's senses, let alone a lad.'

'He's not. He's quite all right.'

'What did he say, then?'

'He just wants to be let alone.'

'So he's left school and gone away with never a word to anyone, just so's he can be alone! That's not sense, Bee lass. That's daft, and he knows it.'

'I don't think he does.'

'Doesn't what?'

'Doesn't know it. He says it as if it was sense.'

'It's not like him. He's a kind lad,' Mrs Earnshaw said, after a pause.

Bee choked.

'What did I say?'

'Said he was kind.'

'That upset you?' her mother asked.

'He is kind really . . .'

'Go on.'

'It's silly. I was going to say, if it had been really him.'

'If he spoke different. And he's behaving different. Did he seem to know you? You couldn't have made a mistake?'

'I know it was him.'

'Was there anything a stranger wouldn't have known?'

'He knew my name. He called me Bee.' But the memory of the expectation with which she had turned to that call, and the distancing coldness of what he said next was too much for her, and she began to cry again.

'You'll have to tell someone,' her mother's voice said, a long way off.

'Who? What do you mean, someone?' But she knew the answer already.

'The chap with a beard that came here that day.'

'No.'

'What good do you think you can do him, lass, by letting him go on like this? It's plain he's not right in his head, let alone in his body.'

'I told you he's not mad. He's perfectly all right. He knows what he's doing,' Bee cried out.

'There's more to talking sense than the words. There's what they mean to you, and if that's different from what they mean to others, then you might as well talk gibberish, it'd come to much the same,' Mrs Earnshaw remarked.

'I can't give him away.'

'It'd be no more giving away than if he was a child or a dumb animal that needs taking care of.'

'He'd never trust me again.'

'Did he tell you where he was living? Or why he'd gone? Did he ask you to keep quiet about seeing him? Did he say anything except that about wanting to be let alone?'

'No.'

'Suppose something happened to him? What'd you feel if you'd kept your mouth shut about this, today, and you could have prevented it by telling the right person?'

Bee moaned.

'I know how you feel about letting him down. But there're times when you have to make up your own mind what's right to do, never mind how much you'll be blamed, or even what you might have promised. I don't say it's easy. Sometimes it seems like setting yourself up against everything you've ever been taught to believe in, and letting down someone you never thought you could.'

'Not if you've promised!' Bee said.

'You may make a promise one day meaning it, that turns out not to be right to be kept another day. I'm not talking about breaking your word just to suit yourself, you know that, Bee. When my father had our Lassie put down because she was half blind and a danger to herself and others, I remember telling him, like you're telling me, that she'd trusted him and he'd broken his promise to her, in a manner of speaking. He said, and I've never forgotten it, "Lassie trusted me to do the best for her, not to do this one thing or the other." That's how you've to think of Thursday. You've to do the best for him, never mind what he says when he's not himself.'

'You talk as if he was crazy!' Bee cried.

'It was you said he wasn't like himself.'

'If I did, what would they do with him?'

'Might see that he doesn't have to lodge with that Molly any more. That'd be a change for the better to start with,' Mrs Earnshaw said, grimly.

'They couldn't put him in prison? Or – anywhere?'

'That'd depend how they find him, I reckon. If he knows what he's at, and can make out a good case for what he's doing, they might leave him, provided he's got somewhere decent to live.'

'They wouldn't take him to hospital?'

'If he's ill he should be looked after. You'll be doing him no kindness if you let him go on like this alone.'

'He wants to be alone.'

'It's not natural for a lad of his age.'

Bee was terribly tired. She couldn't fight any more. She said, 'All right. I'll tell someone. Tomorrow.' She wondered if perhaps this would be one of the promises that when the time came she wouldn't be able to keep.

CHAPTER FOURTEEN

TOMORROW, however, brought no change, and Bee went with her mother to see Mr Tenterden, found for them by Miss Codell. She told him everything, answered all his questions fairly, didn't protest when he pointed out that the police, since they'd already got his description as a missing person, must be informed at once. 'What will they do? Don't let them frighten him, he doesn't like a lot of people at once,' Bee said to the bearded young man. He said, kindly, 'Don't worry. I'll try to arrange to go myself first and have a talk with him before the force arrives on the scene.'

'How will you know him? You haven't ever seen him, have you?' Bee asked.

'Miss Codell's looked me out a photograph from one of the school pictures. It's not very good, but it'll help. Would you like to come along too? It might make him feel better if you were there as well,' Mr Tenterden said.

It was nice of him to ask, it made Bee surer that he didn't mean to hand Thursday over to anyone, police, doctors or anything else, without making sure it was the right thing to do. But Bee didn't want to be there. If she went she'd feel – whatever her mother said – like Judas Iscariot. If she'd been right to betray Thursday for his own good, she certainly didn't mean to be present when he was captured.

She needn't have worried. Thursday wasn't there. Mr Tenterden came round later in the evening, and looking at Bee's startled face, said at once, 'No go, I'm afraid. He never turned up this morning.'

Bee's first feeling was relief.

'The foreman recognized the photograph at once. He hadn't given his own name. Did you know that?' he asked Bee.

'Yes.' Fortunately she didn't have to explain how she knew. She hadn't told anyone of her going on to the site on Saturday.

'One of the men I talked to thought he hadn't come back after the lunch break yesterday afternoon. That would be after he'd seen you, wouldn't it?'

'Yes.' Oh Thursday, what have I done to you? What did I say wrong, that made you not trust me? Perhaps it showed in my eyes that I am a traitor. You knew better than I yesterday that I would tell, so you escaped, like a wild animal that runs when it hears the hunter.

'Did they have an address as well as a name? What about his insurance card?' Mrs Earnshaw asked.

'They had his card, of course, as he hadn't been signed off. I went to the address, but he's never been there. The card wasn't his in the first place, of course.'

'Who'd have thought it? I wonder where he got it from?' Mrs Earnshaw said.

'That shows he's sensible, doesn't it? If there was anything wrong with him, he wouldn't do something clever like that?' Bee said.

'Shows he has brains and knows how to use them,' Mr Tenterden said.

'Then he must be all right.'

'You mustn't count on it,' the young man said gently.

'What do you mean?'

'It can happen that people get disturbed in their feelings, but not in their brains. They can think as well as ever, but what they feel goes wrong.'

'How do you mean, goes wrong?'

'Yes, what do I mean?' the young man asked himself. Bee waited.

'Have you ever been depressed?' he asked her.

'Miserable, d'you mean?'

'Not exactly. Not just miserable about something outside yourself, but hating yourself. Sure you're no good and never will be. Sometimes it comes out of the blue, you don't know why.'

'No. I don't think I have. I get miserable and angry, but not like that.'

'Angry, then. When you're angry, you don't stop thinking, do you? You could still work a double equation, or read the paper and know what it said, your brain wouldn't have given up. But you'd think differently. You'd probably hate things or people you're really quite fond of and you might imagine they were making you angry on purpose, when if you were in your normal state of mind, you'd know that wasn't true.'

'Is Thursday angry?' Bee asked, muddled.

'I don't think so. But I'm not sure that something hasn't upset the way he feels, so that he doesn't behave quite normally.'

'You haven't seen him! You can't tell!' Bee cried.

'Now, Bee! Mr Tenterden's trying to help.'

'He hasn't seen Thursday. I have.'

'Something one of the workmen said reminded me of your description. He said he was a nice enough boy, but you couldn't get near him.'

'He's always been like that. Lynne says he's difficult to get to know,' Bee interrupted.

'It was more than that. Not just shy. This man said it was like talking to a dummy. He said, "All his words came out the same, like those machine men on the telly, as if he'd been taught what to say but didn't know what it ought to mean."'

'That doesn't show anything!'

Mr Tenterden said, 'Is that how he usually talks, Bee?' He hadn't called her by her name before. She suddenly liked him much more than she'd expected. She began to feel she might trust him. She said, 'No. Thursday doesn't talk a lot, but he doesn't talk like a dummy.'

'That way of talking, you'd noticed it too, hadn't you? You said something to me this morning that was rather like what this man said. That the things he said didn't go with the way he said them. Remember?'

'But that doesn't show he's crazy or anything. People talk different at different times.'

'Has he ever been like this before?'

'Not exactly. He goes quiet sometimes, but...' She couldn't finish the sentence.

'I'm going. There's nothing more I can do tonight, and I've got a date.' Suddenly he wasn't a Children's Officer, whatever that was, he was a young man, like Trev, like Thursday would be one day, off for an evening with a girl. Bee wondered if it was Miss Codell. She wouldn't have minded going out with him herself in a year or two's time.

'You'll let us know what happens?' Mrs Earnshaw said, getting up to show him to the door.

'Of course. And if you hear anything of him you'll tell me. You will, won't you? Anything, even if it seems as if it couldn't be important.'

Mrs Earnshaw said, 'Yes,' and moved into the hall, but the young man didn't follow her immediately.

'Bee? You won't try to keep secrets about Thursday, will you? We really must be told anything you know which could possibly help.'

'I've told you everything,' Bee said.

'But if there was anything else. It's important that we should find him as soon as possible. Or if you have any new ideas about where he might be, you should tell us. You do understand that, don't you?'

Bee said, 'Yes.'

'I'll say good night, then. Don't worry too much.'

In bed that night, too hot and too anxious to fall asleep, Bee lay and thought. Her first flash of relief on hearing that Thursday was still free, had been succeeded by a fear which was worse than the fear that she might have betrayed him. At least while he'd been working on the building site, she'd known where he was, if she'd had nightmares about his being ill or dead, she could have gone back to the observation window and seen for herself that he was still in the living world. Or if Mr Tenterden had found him, even if he'd told the police, if he'd been put in a hostel or a hospital, or in a prison, even, she'd know where he was. But now she knew nothing. She didn't know what Thursday would be likely to do, where he'd be likely to go. She had a picture of him as some kind of animal, perhaps hunted, perhaps sick, looking for a hole where he could hide, where no one would find him, where he could lie quiet until his wounds were better and he was fit to face the world again. That was the more hopeful side of her imaginings. At the worst she saw him running, running, desperately, like the hare she'd once seen when she'd been staying with her Aunt Merry, its fur staring, its eyes wild, doing stupid things it'd never have done if it had had its wits about it, taking cover in a field surrounded by dogs and men, inviting its own death. The hare had died horribly, minutes later, and Bee had been sick. She saw Thursday engineering his own fate, asking to be tortured, impaled on his own knowledge, hiding in the one place where he was bound to be discovered.

It was for her to save him. Whatever Mr Tenterden said, whatever the police or all the doctors, psychologists, Children's Officers, School Inspectors, or any one official could say, she was the one who would know what he needed, who would be able to talk in the language he knew. Oh, Thursday, she said, in the sweet summer dark, the stars shining in at her window, and the late moon beginning to rise, I'll be there when you want me, I'll look after you. The dogs shan't get you, somehow I shall hold the men off. Only trust me. I can't bear it when you put me apart, when I, too, become your enemy.

Next day the factory next the bomb site was humming. Of course! It was a weekday, she'd have to be careful no one saw her going through the gap in the boards. But the lane was deserted, except for the car belonging to one of the foremen, Bee supposed, which was often parked up at the blind end. She went right up to it to make sure there wasn't anyone sitting inside watching her, then came back to the hoarding. The factory lunch break was at half past twelve, and she'd left the house at ten, so she had plenty of time before there'd be anyone about. A quick glance down to the bottom of the lane, and she turned to make her way in, and for one bewildering moment thought that she saw the ground of the bomb site purple with blood.

Before she'd actually had the thought, she knew what it was. She climbed through the gap and saw that the willow herb was beginning to flower.

In the ten days since she'd been there last, the place had changed again. More of the rusty iron and the old brick had been covered by the climbing green, the grasses were more than a foot high. There were dandelion clocks – Bee always wondered how anything as solid and earthy as a dandelion flower could turn into those fragile, delicate globes that should have been made by fairies – and white faces on the tall, proud nettles. Mixed with the soot, there was a smell of honey from little pale clovers, growing low. And the willow herb, springing out of chinks in the masonry as well as covering much of the ground, was more pink than purple, and now she looked at it again, not in the least the colour of blood.

Bee went first to the steps and the alcove, but it was undisturbed. No crumbs of food, no dead matches, nothing to show that it had been a place of refuge for a journeying boy. She wandered desolately round the rest of the area, noticing as she went that her feet left imprints on the long damp grass, but that there were no signs of any other feet than her own. Standing in the middle of the site, she called softly, 'Thursday!', knowing he couldn't be hidden anywhere within earshot, knowing that if he were, her voice wouldn't carry above the factory's din. He hadn't been there, she knew it. No one could blame her, then, for having kept quiet about it to Mr Tenterden. But she still couldn't get out of her mind the idea that, like an animal which is being pursued, Thursday might make for familiar ground if he were pushed hard enough. If that were so, it was here he'd come. More than anywhere else, this was his home.

She sat on the steps and wrote on the notepaper pad she'd brought with her. 'Dear Thursday, I know you want to be left alone, but I wanted to tell you you're being looked for. They went to the site where you were working. They don't know where you were staying, and I haven't told anyone about here.'

She hesitated. She wanted to put 'love, Bee'. But how could she say 'love' to a stranger who had told her he didn't want her? She wrote the bare name, 'Bee', folded the paper, put his name outside and wedged it between bricks so that it stuck out into the alcove, you couldn't miss it.

Then, because there was nothing else she could do there, she left.

Coming up into Brigg Street from under the railway bridge, she saw old Mrs Smith with a basket obviously too heavy for her. Bee's first impulse was to pretend she hadn't noticed, to hurry the opposite way. She hadn't forgiven her yet for that last, stupid conversation, it made her hot all over to think of it. But she couldn't do it. The old lady was probably a bit silly anyway, and Thursday had been fond of her. She'd keep her off the subject, talk about the weather or the Queen. It'd only take five minutes anyway.

'I'll take your basket round the corner for you,' she said to the tiny old woman.

'There's kind,' Mrs Smith said, handing it over.

'Gosh, it's heavy!' Bee said, surprised that the old lady had been able to carry it at all.

'Twenty years ago and I'd have taken it from here to the far country and never faltered. That vegetable man, he won't deliver.' And indeed the basket must have held ten pounds of potatoes alone.

'Hot, isn't it?' Bee said, determined to choose the subject of conversation herself.

'Midsummer weather. You'll want to take care.'

'I like it hot. When I was in France last year it was much hotter than this, and I felt fine.'

'Coming up to Midsummer's Eve. That'd be the right time.'

Bee pretended not to hear. It would be about fairies again, she felt sure.

'You may act as if you never heard a word that I'm telling you, but you're listening just the same,' Mrs Smith said, with a little, not unkindly, cackle of laughter. They were just turning the corner into the road of the newspaper shop. She looked up into Bee's face. 'No, you're right, my

137

soul, and I'm wrong. We didn't should've spoken of it out here in the open. Wait till we're in the house, then it's only our own walls have ears.'

'I've got to get home,' Bee said. But she had to walk the old woman to her door, she couldn't just drop the basket and run. And when they reached the shop, the door was open and Mrs Smith walked straight through to the parlour behind. Bee unwillingly followed. Before she'd set the basket down the old woman had shut the door behind her and said, 'You've seen what passes for the lad?'

'What do you mean, "passes for"?'

'It wasn't him, his true self, you'll never tell me?'

'What do you mean?' Bee said again, trembling.

'I can tell you how he was as well as you should tell me. Very quiet, he'd be, and stony. Looking at you with eyes that might never have seen your like before. Talk to you, yes, he'd speak, but in a voice that's lost its music, the way a dead man'd speak, if he could, poor soul. And there'd be you, breaking your heart to get him to answer you back, like a human creature with a bit of feeling, and the red blood running in his veins, and he all the time like a graven image on the other side of the water you'll never get him to cross.'

'How do you know?' Bee asked. She felt for the back of a chair and sat down. The old woman sat on the other side of the little table and looked at her.

'You're thinking, chance there's sense in what I'm telling you now, my soul? Now you've seen for yourself how they go about things and the way they are?'

'You've seen him too?' Bee asked, feeling as if all her breath had been knocked out of her.

'Not since he was taken.'

'Then how do you *know*?' Bee cried again.

'I've seen a plenty, child, in my time. He's not the first,

nor he'll not be the last, the Lord save us. I've seen babies took like it in their cradles, that never gave their Mams a smile nor spoke a word of any Christian tongue. I've seen children taken, that had laughed and sported with their kind and then fell dumb and silly, sitting picking at a piece of cloth in a corner by the hearth till you could have struck them for the weariness of it, hadn't you known better than to lift your hand against one of them. I've seen grown men, and women too, come back so their own children didn't know them, with their poor eyes starting from their heads with what they'd seen and their mouths locked up for telling a mortal soul about it.'

'I don't understand! You mean crazy? Thursday's not mad!' Bee said.

'I didn't say mad, my heart. I said took.'

'You said that before. I don't believe in fairies,' was what Bee meant to say, but before she'd reached the last word, Mrs Smith had leant across the table and put her hand over Bee's mouth.

'It's you that's mad, girl bach. To say the name out loud like that. And if you're thinking, as there's many do, that down here in the city they're not about because there's no green, look what's happened to the lad in the roads and streets around us. It's not rings they need, nor hillocks, though they'll use them likely, if they're there for the using. What should houses and the slippery black roads mean to them, that was there when the place was fields and meadows? Give them a blade of grass or a buttercup stalk and they'll be out, seeking for what they need, be it a nurse woman to help with a birth or a fiddler to play at a wedding.'

She didn't look mad. She didn't even sound so old, talking quick and sharp and clear, but perhaps this was how old people got when they were going a bit crazy. Bee tried to feel sorry, as if she were talking to Nancy along the road, who had never grown up, but ran about in short socks, with her hair done up with ribbons and her clothes a little girl's clothes, but whose buttony face was wrinkled and whose hair, you saw when you got near, was going grey. The trouble was that Mrs Smith didn't have Nancy's sweet, stupid look, and her words weren't at all like Nancy's careful slow speech. Bee said kindly, 'If you're right about all those people being – taken, like you say, what happens to them next? I mean, if they'd really been taken away, how do they get back again?'

'That's their images, my soul. What's put in their place.'

'I don't understand.'

'Child, you've heard of changelings, surely?'

'Something to do with babies,' Bee said stupidly.

'When there's a newborn babe that hasn't had the priest's blessing, or that's without a name, priest or no priest, they can take it and put one of their own in its place. That's the child that never smiles nor gives, it's take, take, take, for as long as the day will last. Eggshells.'

'Eggshells?'

'Brewing ale in eggshells, that's what'll make it laugh. Make it laugh and you've spoiled the spell. Didn't you know, my soul, if you can make him laugh he's yours?'

'I don't know anything like that.'

'That's the babies. Later, they'll take them for a purpose. To mend a shoe, maybe, or to give them a tune. Your lad had a grand hand with the banjo, wasn't it? Or was it the harp?'

'The guitar,' Bee said, a little stiffly.

'That'd be the tune they'd want him to play. They open the hill for him, you see, and before he knows what he's at, he's inside, playing at the feast and believing the time that's passing is in minutes by the clock. While for us outside it's hours and days, maybe weeks and years he's been away. Time's different there, with them. What's a second to them's a dreary lifetime to one of us.'

'Then –? But if he's there, how can he be here? He is here, I've seen him.'

'What you've seen's the stock, child. Didn't your Mam have told you any tales of the good people? She's from the city then, and trusting in stones and walls to keep them away?'

'Mum came from the North. She lived in the country.' Bee wanted to say that her mother didn't believe in fairies either, but the memory of the tale about her grandmother's vision held her back.

'There's a plenty about in the North, I've heard,' the old woman said.

'What's a stock, anyway?'

'An image they make out of their own stuff. Made so it's that like the true Christian soul you can't tell the difference, wasn't it for the cruel spiteful ways they have on them.'

'But what do they do?'

'Whatever the one that was taken did, without it was work that might help others or give any poor soul a sight of joy.'

Bee looked at the old woman opposite her. She saw the long, clever nose, the kind wrinkles round the eyes bright with intelligence, the good mouth, and she thought, 'She's not crazy! She's not even silly-old! She believes what she's saying. Mum said fairies was another way of explaining what you don't understand. No one understands what's happened to Thursday, why he's gone off like this, why he's different. She's seen other people like this. She said, cruel and spiteful, and that's what he was when he told me I was ugly, and it isn't like the real him. Perhaps she knows. Perhaps she'd tell me what to do to help.' She thought of what

Lynne had told her —'the only person who'd be able to get him back' old Mrs Smith had said, and she'd meant Bee, or Lynne had thought she did. And what had she said to embarrass Lynne? Bee wanted to know.

She said, cautiously, 'Isn't there anything you can do? I mean, does the real person ever come back?'

'If you can break the spell, girl-bach. Certain nights is better than others. Midsummer's Eve, that's what I was telling you.'

'When's that?'

'There's ignorance! You'll be telling me you don't know the days of the week next. The twenty-fourth day of this month, that's Midsummer's Day, and the night before, they'll be about. That'll be the chance.'

'What do you have to do?'

'Make them cross the water with him, that's one way, but I doubt that'd be hard. Cry out at them with a holy name, that's another. Some take silver and buy the soul back, but it's tricky work bargaining with them, and if it's less than thirty pieces they can take him back and the money's like withered leaves in the buyer's hand. Catch one of them in a pint pot and make them give the lad back as the price you're asking, but that's not easy either. I've heard of folks sprinkling them with the holy water when they're at their revels, but if you miss out more than one or two, their power's too great and all you'll do is to anger them, while what you need's to please them. Have you got a sweet voice?'

'What?' Bee asked, bewildered.

'Are you a singer, girl? Have you the gift of melody?'

'No. Trev says I sound like a barn owl hooting.'

'If you had, you might have sung to them and earned him as your pay for delighting them.'

'I couldn't,' Bee said at once.

'Best not try, then. And the holy name's no help without it comes from the heart. Do you belong to the chapel? Or church, maybe?'

'Not really. None of us really belong.'

'Say your prayers?' the old woman asked.

'N-no. No.'

'Some need them, others don't. But don't you be calling on the name of God then. They'll know if it's on the lips only. Let me think what you should do when all these ways is no use to you.'

'You said, make him laugh.'

'It could be hard, a lad of his years. That's for the babes that haven't started out of the cradle and don't know the wicked ways of the world.'

'There must be another way,' Bee urged.

'It's difficult.'

'I could try.'

'There'll be danger in it.'

'I could pretend I was brave.'

'It'll bring pain. Not to you only, to them around you.'

'What is it?'

'You've to hold him the night through till the bird brings in the morning. You've to hold him against them and their tricks and their temptings. You've to hold him against his own wish and longing, for with the lad like he is, all he'll know will be that it's his heart's desire to go back to the forgetting and the singing and the dancing.'

'Hold him how?'

'Any way you can.'

'Where?'

'You don't need me to tell you.'

'Just me? Alone?'

'Others'd be a hindrance, no help to ye at all,' the old woman said.

'Me? Does it have to be me?'

'You're the only one,' Mrs Smith said, as she'd said it to Lynne.

'Why? Why me?'

'You know the answer to that too, dear heart.'

Bee said out loud what she didn't think she'd ever have said out loud to anyone. 'Because I'm the one that loves him.'

CHAPTER FIFTEEN

IT was extraordinary to come back to her mother's ordinary kitchen with stories of fairies and spells still in her ears. During the week that followed, Bee felt confused, as if she, like Thursday, were living in two places at once, one the familiar, everyday world, and another, only half understood, in which nothing was to be expected, anything might happen. She found herself seeing things in a different light, looking at places and people around her with a different sort of explanation in her mind for their presence and their behaviour. She had a frightening fantasy one day that no one she saw was what they appeared to be, no one was his true self, as if all the human qualities had disappeared, leaving only the husks of real people, miming kindness, pity, affection, but cold as death underneath. She was half terrifying herself, half enjoying her fear, when Jean dropped in for a chat, and the sight of her, so completely alive, so much all of a piece, brought Bee up sharp. Jean was exactly what she seemed to be, couldn't possibly be anything else. There might be people who put on an act of being something quite different from what they felt, but as long as there were others like Jean about, Bee could be sure that there was also warmth and reality.

'When's the baby due, Jean?' she asked, not because she didn't know if she stopped to think, but to say something showing her interest.

'Ten days. Tuesday week, the twenty-second. Might be early, though. You never know your luck.'

'They say if it's early it's a boy,' Mrs Earnshaw said.

'Lot of old wives' tales. You can't believe half of what they say,' Jean said.

'Don't you believe old wives' tales ever?' Bee asked.

'Not to say believe. All the same, there's things I wouldn't do, if you can understand what I mean. Ladders, for instance. You don't want to chance your luck when you're carrying, that's what I say.'

'That's right,' Bee's mother said.

'Do you think babies ever get taken?' Bee asked.

'What d'you mean, taken?'

'I meant sort of changed. So they aren't like ordinary children.'

'What's that got to do with taking? Kidnapped, you mean?'

Bee gave up. She saw that she'd never be able to say what she meant without seeming either babyish or mad.

'Which do you want, Jean? A boy or a girl?'

'It'll be a boy, you see. But I don't really mind. As long as it's got all its fingers and toes I'll settle for it.'

Bee wished it was she who was having the baby. She envied Jean her certainty, her safety. If you were Jean, just going to have a baby by a husband you loved, if you were Jean, safe and happy, and sure that having this baby was going to bring happiness to everyone all round you, you could get on with living, you could just be you. Jean didn't have to worry where Trev was, what he was thinking, how his mind worked. She was cocooned in a process as old as life and as valuable. No one could say to Jean, 'You're no good, you're not *doing* anything.' Jean was producing a new human being. Almost everyone agreed that this was something worth doing.

At the week-end the doctor came and pronounced Bee fit to go back to school. She was to take it easy for the first week or two. 'If you find you're getting tired out by the end of the morning, you'll just have to come home and go to bed. I'll write you a note for your headmaster,' he said to Bee.

'I'll be all right.'

'You can't tell. Learning's a tiring process and you're out of practice, remember.'

Her first morning at school wasn't at all what Bee had expected. She'd known she'd be lost in the lessons; the class seemed to have got through more in the weeks she'd been away than in the whole of the rest of the year. But what she hadn't realized was how little used she was to being with other people. She'd never noticed before how everyone in the school shouted. They had to, to make themselves heard above the noises that went on all the time, noises of feet, of desks banging, of doors shutting, of voices. Not only that, they all moved so quickly, there were so many of them. Bee couldn't move her eyes fast enough to follow all their movements, it made her giddy.

'Is it always like this?' she said to Lynne in the lunch break.

'Like what?'

'Does everyone move about so much? And talk so quickly?'

'It's no different from ordinary. It's because you've been away so long, you've forgotten what it's like.'

'I can't think how I never noticed it before.'

'Have a biscuit?' Lynne said.

'No thanks. I'm not hungry.'

'Has Alison told you about the play?'

'No.'

'You have got to be Hermia. I told you so.'

'When? I mean, when're we suppose to be doing it?'

'Not till nearly the end of term. Alison wanted to do it

on Midsummer's Eve, but Miss Stevens said no it would upset everyone's work too much, and it wasn't fair on the "O" level people and all that. It'd have been next week, you see.'

'Who are you going to be?'

'Snug. Doesn't it sound crazy? I suppose he meant it to.'

'Who's Snug?'

'A joiner, whatever that is. Doesn't have hardly anything to say. He's Lion when they act their play. Just roars.'

'Who's being Lysander?'

'Timmy. And one thing Alison has been clever about, I must say. She's got Marigold being Puck, and Peter Dinsley for Oberon.'

'I'd never thought of the fairies being coloured,' Bee said.

'It's dead right, though. After all, they ought to be different somehow. Claire's going to make up dark too, and we're borrowing Asru Lal from the lower thirds, for the little Indian boy.'

'I still think it's stupid. If we had to do a Shakespeare, why couldn't we do one we don't know? The *Midsummer Night's Dream*'s the one absolutely everyone's seen some time or other.'

'It hasn't got so many rude bits in it as the others. Except the histories, of course, and who wants to do them? PETER!' Lynne bawled suddenly across the playground, making Bee's head spin with the unaccustomed noise.

'What?' Peter yelled back.

'Come over here and tell Bee about the play.'

Peter came over and started at once, declaiming.

> 'Thou remember'st
> Since once I sat upon a promontory
> And heard a mermaid, on a dolphin's back,
> Uttering such dulcet and harmonious breath,

> That the rude sea grew civil at her song,
> And certain stars shot madly from their spheres,
> To hear the sea maid's musick.'

'He's good, isn't he?' Lynne said.

'Fantastic.'

Bee realized suddenly that she'd never really listened to the play before. She'd seen it acted, she'd read bits of it, she'd even, once, very long ago, been one of the attendant court ladies in the first and last scenes. She knew it was written in blank verse because everyone always said so, but she'd never heard it as verse for herself. And now, unexpectedly, she did. Peter was West Indian, and he spoke with an accent and an intonation that was certainly not English. Perhaps it was because of this that Bee heard words she'd never noticed before, and in Peter's soft singing voice, she heard the music of the lines, and thought, in astonishment, 'It's poetry! It's not just a play about a silly mix-up in a wood, and a man with a donkey's head, and elves and things posturing about all over the place. It actually means something. It's about the country, English country, not Athens, English workmen practising for a Bank Holiday competition, boys and girls quarrelling about who went with who, just like the upper forms at school, and – English fairies?'

Peter went on.

> 'Why should Titania cross her Oberon?
> I do but beg a little changeling boy
> To be my henchman.'

Bee stopped listening. She went away, miles away, away into a dark passage of her own thoughts. She was woken out of it again by the realization that Peter had stopped speaking. She had no idea what he had been saying in the last few minutes.

'Super,' Lynne said, with warm admiration for what she couldn't at all do herself.

'Super,' Bee echoed, knowing she must say something, and unable to think of anything original.

'Wake up, Bee! You look as if Peter'd hypnotized you or something.'

'What's hypnotized?' Peter asked.

'It's when you get someone to do what you tell them without them really knowing. Sort of like casting a spell, only this is all scientific. People can get hypnotized so they don't know they're having their teeth out, or babies, or anything.'

'In my home some peoples believe in spells,' Peter said.

'Honestly? Lots of people do?'

'Ignorant peoples. Peoples who have not been to school.'

'What sort of spells?'

'Some of them are good, some of them are bad. You can buy medicines for many things. You don't have so much medicines here.'

'Like what?'

'To pass examination, perhaps. Or to make a person love you.'

'You've never bought one of those, I suppose?' Lynne asked, teasing.

Peter said, seriously, 'No.'

'Would you? If you wanted something the medicine was supposed to do for you?'

'Perhaps I would. Perhaps I would not.'

'Do you think the spells might really work?' Bee asked.

'In my country I think they are working. I don't think they are working here,' Peter said.

'Why not?'

'Is too cold. Too many houses. Too much cleverness.'

Lynne roared with laughter.

'Peter, you're tremendous! Isn't he, Bee?'

'Bee doesn't like what I say.'

'Don't you, Bee? Why not?'

'It isn't that I don't like it. I was just thinking.'

'She wants to buy a medicine to make her pass exams.' There was no sting in Lynne's teasing. She hadn't said, 'to make a person love her', because she knew this was the focus point of Bee's anxiety. Lynne was kind.

By the end of the morning, Bee was exhausted.

'You'd better go home,' Lynne said.

'It seems so feeble.'

'But if your doctor said? Come on. I'll go with you to say you want to leave.'

In the office Antonia Codell was typing. As they opened the door she jammed two keys together and said, 'Damn!'

'Miss Codell!'

'Bee! Did you come because –' She checked herself. 'Can I do something for you?'

'I've got a letter for Mr Stanton.'

'Urgent? He's got somebody in with him just at the moment, but I could interrupt.'

'It's from my doctor. He said I wasn't to stay all day if I got tired.'

'Of course. You've only just come back, haven't you? How does it feel?'

'It's all right. Much louder than I'd remembered.'

'And you're tired. I'll take the letter in straight away.'

She came back almost immediately. 'Mr Stanton says, of course, go home now or after dinner, whichever you feel like. And he says you'd better see how you feel the rest of the week, and don't bother to ask, just leave when you've had enough.'

'Thanks,' Bee said.

'Anything else?'

'You said when I came in, had I come for something. What was it, please?'

'I thought you might have come to ask about Thursday Townsend.'

'What about him?' Bee asked, wishing her legs felt stronger.

'Where he was . . .'

'Do you *know*?' Bee cried out.

'Hasn't Brian . . . Hasn't Mr Tenterden been to see you?'

'What's happened?'

'He was coming to see you this morning.'

'What's happened to Thursday?'

'Don't look like that, Bee. They've found him. He's safe.'

'Where?'

'I'm not quite sure. In a hospital, I think.'

'He's ill!'

'I don't think so. Not exactly.'

'Why didn't someone tell me at once, when it happened?'

'Mr Tenterden was coming to see you this morning. He didn't know you'd be coming back to school.'

'Has he seen Thursday?'

'Yes.'

'How was he? What was he like? What's been happening to him?'

'You'd better go home, I think. He might just still be there,' Miss Codell said. She looked as if she'd have liked to say more but wasn't quite ready to.

Bee went without saying goodbye. Half an hour earlier she'd wondered how she was going to walk home, but now she stumbled, half running, her heart racing, everything inside her ticking restlessly like a time bomb in anxiety and anger. She burst into the house and saw her mother, in the kitchen as usual, alone.

'Where's Mr Tenterden?'

'Went about an hour ago.'

'What did he say about Thursday? Where is he?'

'In hospital. Somewhere out in the country.'

'What's wrong with him? Miss Codell said he wasn't ill.'

'He's not ill like you're thinking. It's like Mr Tenterden was saying the other day. He's not well in his mind.'

Bee sat down on a chair.

'I feel awful.'

'You've been running.'

'I thought I might catch Mr Tenterden. Miss Codell at school said he was coming here.'

'Poor lass.'

'Don't *sympathize*. If you do I'll cry, and I don't want to.'

'Have a drink.'

'Yes, please. Not hot. Water or something.'

Mrs Earnshaw put a glass of orange squash down by Bee.

'When it's this weather I do sometimes think we should have a fridge.'

'It'd be nice. Would Dad?'

'If I asked he'd get me one. Trouble is there's other things to come out of his money first. If you gollop like that, Bee, you'll give yourself hiccups.'

'Could I have some more?'

Mrs Earnshaw filled her glass.

'Not but what if you let the tap run long enough it does come up nice and cold.'

'Mum! What did Mr Tenterden say? I want to know everything he said.'

'I'll do my best. They found him last week-end.'

'How?'

'Seems the police had told the Labour Exchanges and the places that take on chaps to work on demolition to look out for him.'

'It was my fault then. I gave him away.'

'I said before, Bee, if you want to do what's best for him, you can't go on any promises you made to a poor lad that's out of his wits.'

'He's not!'

'You know better than the doctors?'

'He wasn't doing anyone any harm.'

'What about himself, then?'

'He wasn't hurting himself.'

Mrs Earnshaw looked at Bee without answering for a moment. Then she said, 'You've to see Mr Tenterden.'

'Why? When?'

'He asked if you'd go round to his office in the Pendlebury Road after tea.'

'Do you know what he wants to see me for?'

Mrs Earnshaw hesitated again.

'Is there a lot more you haven't told me?' Bee asked.

'Not that he's said. It was me asked him if he hadn't better see you himself. I knew there'd be things you'd want to ask that I couldn't answer. It's best you should hear direct whatever there is to say.'

Bee trembled. The kitchen spun round her, and she shut her eyes and held on to the sides of the hard wooden chair. Mr Tenterden was going to tell her that Thursday was mad. She would never see him again. She remembered a cold, flat voice saying, 'You look ugly when you cry.' Thursday in his right mind would never have said that to her. She hurt her fingers by the desperate grip she held of the chair, and the hard smooth, sane feeling of the wood was as if she were holding on to reality. Because in a world where someone you knew and trusted turned away from you, how could you tell which of you it was that had changed, or who you yourself were?

'Bee,' said her mother's voice.

Bee opened her eyes.

'Why not go upstairs and have a lie-down on your bed? You can eat later, if you want, before you go round to see Mr Tenterden.'

Bee said, 'All right,' with wooden lips. The kitchen had stopped spinning round and she got upstairs without difficulty. She kicked off her shoes and lay on top of the coverlet of the bed. She'd expected that she'd cry when she was alone, but to her surprise she didn't want to. She lay, dry-eyed, looking at the ceiling, which had one of those unstartling patterns of white on white, which don't force themselves on your attention but which you can follow if you want to. This one was geometric, lines following each other up and down, from side to side within a square. Each square made a sort of maze. Bee had often wandered in the squares with her mind and her eyes, trying to get in, trying to get out. She walked in them now, without meaning to, and, as usual, found the first two – starting from the stain where the rain had come in through the roof – easy, and the third impossible. There wasn't a way in. The lines, faintly shiny on a dull background, were hopelessly misleading. Every now and then Bee's eyelids dropped and she started awake again. The seventh time it happened, they stayed shut. Bee slept.

She dreamed that she was inside the third maze. She had a moment of triumph at having found the way in, followed by a feeling of sick fear. She was at the centre, and outside someone, or something, was trying to get in. She could hear movements which were still distant, but which would come nearer. If she had solved the puzzle of the maze, so could the person who was now outside, and she knew, as one does know without being able to tell how, in dreams, that when he found her he would do something terrible to her.

The centre, where she stood, was a square, surrounded by tall white houses, with blind, shuttered windows and narrow, closed doors. Between them, straight roads led off in different directions, all nameless and all ending in rightangled turns of T-junctions. The roads were guarded by more white, secret houses. Bee stood and trembled. She heard the feet outside stepping round and round the periphery of the maze, as if their owner were looking for the way which could lead him in.

Bee ran. She ran down one road and up another, terrified. She didn't think where she was going. Any way was as dangerous as any other, because she didn't know where her pursuer might go. She ran blindly, always followed by the panic of being hunted. And the running was dream running, her feet were clogged as if by mud, each step cost an enormous effort, she moved very, very slowly. When she stopped, exhausted, she heard the footsteps of the other person in the maze, now quite close, it seemed, only just on the other side of the nearest white wall. Bee shrieked. All that came out was her breath, soundless. But as if he'd heard that silent cry, the person on the other side of the wall stopped walking, and when he started again, the dream changed. He walked as Thursday walked. Bee recognized his steps.

She was still frightened. She hadn't recovered from the fear of the unknown stranger. She had to absorb the understanding that the hunter was Thursday; he must discover that she, his quarry, was Bee. The footsteps went walking round and round, and never getting closer, and Bee realized suddenly that the house faces were shams, hollow; there were no rooms behind them, they were paper thin. They were pretending to be the outsides of houses, of homes where people lived. Instead the whole maze was made of nothing but walls, with blind windows which could look only from one road into another. She had somehow to let Thursday know she was there. She called his name, 'Thursday!' But her voice came out hardly more than a whisper which echoed back from all those blank walls around her. She went to the side where his footsteps had last sounded, and drummed on the wall with her hands. But it was like banging against a wall padded with cotton wool. There was no sound. Somehow she had to attract his attention and let him know that these walls were fake, that there was no brick or stone separating them. She called, softly, his name, 'Thursday!' It came out like a song, a visible melody, which floated up out of her enclosed street, over the walls, like a bright bird. She saw and heard his answering, 'Bee!' There was a tearing, a rending, and for the moment she was seized with panic, as a great hole appeared in the wall nearest to her, and a dark figure burst through. It seemed the figure of a stranger, and she wanted to get away from it; at the same time she knew who it was and wished to welcome him. She was torn between fear and love and cried out with the pain of it. She heard her own cry as she woke.

CHAPTER SIXTEEN

MR Tenterden had a very little room as an office. There was a dark green filing cabinet, a table covered with paper, two calendars on the walls, and three desks, each with a telephone. Mr Tenterden's desk had a bowl with two roses swimming in it. Otherwise it was as businesslike as the others.

'Bee? I'm glad to see you. Sit down,' he said.

Bee sat.

'Your mother's told you that Thursday Townsend has been found?'

Bee said, 'Yes.'

'Did she tell you any more?'

'Why's he in hospital? He's not mad or anything,' Bee said.

'There wasn't any choice, Bee.'

'He could have come to us. Mum would have had him, I know she would.'

'She might. But it wouldn't have been fair to ask her, with Thursday in this state.'

'What state?'

'He's very disturbed, Bee. He's absolutely silent. He's very withdrawn. He wouldn't say a word.'

Bee was silent too.

'The doctor who examined him thinks that he may be having a sort of nervous breakdown.'

'What sort of nervous breakdown?'

'No one can tell till he's been in hospital for a bit longer.'

'Will he have to stay there long?'

'It'll depend on how he is. He'll have to stay there for the moment, there's no doubt of that.'

'Can't I see him?' Bee asked, and immediately wondered if she could bear to.

'It would be a great help if you would,' Mr Tenterden said.

'Help?'

'There's no one who knows Thursday as well as you do. The doctor there rang me up this morning and I suggested you would be the person he might like to see.'

'What for?'

'They have to know whether he's changed, and if so how much.'

'I suppose I could tell them that.'

'I can't get away till the week-end. I could take you down then.'

'Is it far?'

'About thirty miles outside London. Perhaps a bit more.'

'This hospital –' Bee said, and stopped.

'Yes?'

'Are the other people there mad?'

'They have all sorts. I don't think you'd be likely to see the worst cases.'

'Would Thursday?'

'I don't think so. They generally try to keep the more seriously ill people apart from the others.'

'What's the difference between having a nervous break-down and being mad?'

'You're thinking too black and white, Bee.'

'What do you mean?' Bee asked, surprised.

'Madness isn't a definite thing like that. It isn't like having measles or not. It's a question of reality, really.'

'I don't understand.'

'I don't suppose any two of us would agree exactly

159

about what's real, or what isn't. If someone sees the world a little differently from the rest of us, that's all right, as long as it doesn't upset the way we live. We just think he's a bit odd. But if all his ideas are different, if what he thinks makes nonsense of what we believe's true, then we do get upset. It's a sort of threat against us, do you see?'

'You mean, that's when we'd say he was mad?'

'That's right.'

'But if it's like that, it might be us that was mad, not him.'

'It could be, couldn't it? But there are more of us.'

'That can't be all! There must be something else!' Bee cried.

'Sometimes a person's ideas make him dangerous.'

'Thursday's not dangerous.'

Mr Tenterden said, 'I know it sounds ridiculous, Bee, when you know someone as well as you know Thursday. But it can happen. People can change.'

In Bee's inside ear she heard another voice, a soft, lilting voice, that said, 'An image they make out of their own stuff. Make it so it's that like the true Christian soul you can't tell the difference, wasn't it for the cruel, spiteful ways they have on them.' To Mr Tenterden she said, 'I see.'

He sat looking at her across the desk. He was waiting for her to say whether she'd come or not. Instead, she touched the roses and said, 'They're nice. I like them.'

'I was given them yesterday,' Mr Tenterden said.

'Miss Codell gave them to him,' Bee thought. She looked at Mr Tenterden, who was looking at the roses, his mind far away from her and from Thursday, and she wondered what he and Miss Codell said to each other, whether they were really in love; how proper lovers, grown-up lovers, behaved. What did they do when they were alone together? Did they kiss, or what? Bee envied them for being older than she was, for knowing all the things she still had to find out. She envied Miss Codell the look on Mr Tenterden's face. Thursday wouldn't be thinking about her like that, he was locked up in another world where she wasn't his lover, wasn't his friend. He might even think of her as his enemy. The voice in her mind's ear said, 'You've to hold him the night through ... against their tricks and their temptings ...', and her heart swelled till it felt large enough to contain Thursday's coldness, his indifference, even his hate, and she said abruptly, startling the young man opposite to her, lost in his own longing fancy, 'I want to see Thursday. If you'll take me at the week-end, I'll come.'

CHAPTER SEVENTEEN

IT was a long week. Bee was generally tired and always preoccupied. She tried to work, but she had lost the trick of concentration. Besides this, the desire to sleep would suddenly overcome her at surprising and unsuitable moments. And always, whether she was trying to understand the principles of solid geometry, or the economic policy of Parliament under Sir Robert Peel, or to memorize the principal exports of Amsterdam (who on earth would want to have that bit of knowledge by heart when they grew up?), or Hermia's lines in *A Midsummer Night's Dream*, always there was a part of her attention which was occupied with something quite different. It was engaged in a hospital somewhere outside London, where people behaved extraordinarily because they saw the ordinary world through the distorting glass of their fantastic imaginations. Or because somehow or other their true selves had been stolen from them, and all that was left was a body, mechanically going through the motions of being real, but having no more to do with the whole person than a plastic flower has to do with the tender shoots of spring.

In the middle of the week, Bee went round to the newspaper shop on her way home after school. Because it was hot, both doors were standing open, the one into the street, and the inner door behind the shop. When her eyes got accustomed to the sudden dimness, Bee saw the person she had come to look for, sitting at the table in the back room. The younger Mr Smith was behind the counter, stacking up cartons of cigarettes. He nodded to her.

'Evening. You better?' he said.

'Yes, thanks.'

'Suppose you've heard they've found your boy friend?'

'Yes.'

'Too bad he's been taken ill like that. Must have been a shock for you.'

'Ill?' Bee said.

'Some sort of breakdown, I heard. In hospital, isn't he?'

'Yes.'

'You never know, do you? One of the best boys on the round, too. Can't get anyone to do it like he did.'

Bee said nothing.

'You don't want to worry too much. Wonderful what they do nowadays for that sort of nervous trouble. Uncle of a friend of mine was really bad, crying all day long, and miserable. Couldn't hardly speak. Religious with it, too. They put some sort of electric current through his brain, and after a treatment or two he lost all that.'

'Electric current?' Bee asked, horrified.

'Not much. Just a little. Stirs the brain up, the doctor said. Makes it work a different way.'

'And he was all right afterwards? I mean, was he?' Bee asked.

'Bit forgetful. Couldn't make up his mind about things sometimes. They used to laugh at him a bit, taking half an hour to choose whether it was to be a pint of ale or a half of bitter. But he didn't go round talking about hell. Not near so much of a Woeful Willie he wasn't, after he'd had the shocks.'

Bee stared at him.

'Is that the girl? Let her come here and speak with me,' old Mrs Smith said from the back room, and in a sort of daze, Bee went. She sat down at the table and looked at the little old woman helplessly, unable to speak, longing for reassurance.

'Don't listen to his words, my soul. Though he's my own son, he hasn't the gift. He sees what lies beneath his nose and that's the whole of it, for him.'

Bee sat in the small dark room and felt her pulses slow down and her mind begin to work again. She said, 'Thursday. They've put him in hospital.'

'That's how it often is, child, for want of understanding.'

'I'm to see him at the week-end.'

'Where?' the old woman asked sharply.

'Somewhere in the country. Outside London.'

'That's no good,' the old woman said.

'What do you mean?'

'He has to come back through the same door he went by. You've to get him to London, girl, for it's from London they took him, and it'll be to London they must bring him back.'

'How –?'

'Girl, bach, you've to use your wits. Your wits and your heart that's telling you now the very corner of this great city where you and he will have the combat that's to save him.'

Bee said, 'What will I do? I don't know what's right to do. I don't understand. I don't know anything.'

'You don't have to know, lassie. All you've to do is to let your heart lead your head. You've to look for the time when the holy bird calls in the morning, for that's when they're at their weakest, and you've the chance of holding him. You've to get him to want to come with you, my soul, and that's the hardest part of it all, for they've sweet ways with them, and their ladies are fine and lovely, and their music is such as would wind the wool off the ewe's back or make the songbird give them her eggs out of the very nest she's warming.'

Bee sat and looked at the old woman as if she could take in all she needed to know through her eyes.

'What's your given name, my heart? The lad never calls you by it when he's speaking of you.'

'Bee.'

'Was you called by the priest at your coming? You needn't tell me, I can read the signs. You've grown with the knowledge and with the love as that poor lad never had all the years of his life. I doubt you'll not be in mortal danger. Was you frightened, then?'

To anyone else Bee would have said, 'No.' To this extraordinary old woman she said the truth. 'Yes.'

The old woman nodded. 'It's right you should be. It's the lad that never knew fear was the one most likely to be took. You'll go to him with terror and you'll stay by him with terror, and terror will sharpen your wits and brighten your eyes, and give you the power to save him.'

Bee said desperately, 'I still don't know what I'm supposed to do.'

'You'll know on the heartbeat, my soul.'

'How will I? How will I *know*?'

'You've to learn to listen to the meaning behind the words, and the music behind the notes and the tokening of silence. Don't be quick to speak or too ready with your understanding. When you know what to know, hold fast and never loosen your hold till what you want's in your arms and there to stay.'

She stopped abruptly. Bee saw that she was being dismissed and got up to go.

'Thank you.'

'And don't you be forgetting the rowan tree.'

'What rowan tree?'

Mrs Smith's eyes closed. Her face seemed to shut up, she looked like a small figure carved out of ivory. Bee looked at her for a moment longer, then left.

'What's rowan?' she said to her mother that night.

'I'm glad your grandfather can't hear you ask that. To hear one from the north ask what's rowan?'

'You're from the north, I'm not. What is it, then?'

'Ash. Mountain ash. All over the fells behind where we lived. White flowers in the spring, flat, like a wedding posy, red berries in the autumn. Orange red, sunset colour.'

'I see! The oak and the ash!'

'That's right.'

'What's magic about it?'

'Nowt that I've ever heard of,' Mrs Earnshaw said flatly.

'I'd an auntie used to put a sprig of ash over the door for luck,' Jean said.

'Why?'

'Like I said, for luck.'

'Like a horseshoe?'

'That's right.'

'What else?'

'What do you mean, what else?'

'Did she do anything else for luck like that?'

'Not that I know of. Except she wore a string of blue glass beads round her middle against the rheumatics.'

'Did it work?'

'It didn't make her any better, if that's what you mean, because she never did have the rheumatics anyway.'

'Perhaps the beads kept them away.'

'That's what she said.'

'Coming round dinner-time Sunday, Jean?' Mrs Earnshaw asked.

'If I'm still around. Saw another doctor yesterday. That makes eight. Never the same one twice.'

'What did he say?'

'Said I should go back again Friday.'

'What's that for?' Mrs Earnshaw asked sharply.

'My ankles've been swelling a bit. Don't look like that, Trev's Mum. It's only the heat. Except for that, I'm fine.'

'Feel all right in yourself?'

'Bit tired sometimes. You know.'

'You'll be glad when it's over, now,' Mrs Earnshaw said.

'Can't wait. I'd better go. Trev's jumpy. If I'm not back before he gets in, he's sure I've had the baby in the street. I said to him yesterday, "Trev," I said, "you don't have babies like that, so quick you can't get inside somewhere," and he said, "After what they told us at that class for fathers about relaxation and that, I've come to the conclusion you're so relaxed you won't have time to get to the nearest lamp-post." Just as if I was a little dog!'

'Better not go too far afield.'

'I don't. I'm even shopping at Porritt's, though I like the Co-op ever so much better.'

'That's right. You do that. There's not all that much difference really.'

'I know. It's all in the mind. 'Bye Trev's Mum, be seeing you. 'Bye, Bee. See you Sunday, maybe.'

'I won't be here,' Bee said.

'How come?'

'I'm going with Mr Tenterden . . .'

'New boy friend?'

'He's taking me to see Thursday.'

'Sorry, Bee!'

'You're going, then?' Mrs Earnshaw asked.

'Mr Tenterden says the doctor wants to see me. He's coming to fetch me Sunday morning early.'

'Want to take lunch?'

'One of your picnics, Mum? That'd be super.' For a moment Bee had a pang of pure, greedy, childish pleasure. As a family they didn't often have picnics, but when they did they were good ones. Her mother had a gift for packing just the right combination of tastes and consistencies. There was always a surprise, and the picnics were never all the same, each one was different. It would be fun to share a meal like this with Mr Tenterden, to show off her Mum's genius.

'Hope your Thursday gets better quickly,' Jean said at the door.

'Thanks.'

'Look after yourself. Let me know what your doctor says, Friday,' Mrs Earnshaw called after Jean.

Jean came back a step in order to say, 'I can tell you what he'll say, now. "Coming along nicely, Mrs er ... Mother. Let's just make sure there's plenty of room for the head," he says, and then he squeezes my stomach down as if he was going to pop the baby out like an orange out of a Christmas stocking. It doesn't hurt, I must admit, that, though. Funny what they can do, isn't it?'

Jean was wrong. Trevor came in on Friday evening to tell them that the doctor said she had got raised blood pressure and she was to be kept in hospital. 'Nothing to worry about,' he'd said, but Trevor did worry. Bee saw by the shadow that came across her mother's face that she didn't take the doctor's words as completely reassuring.

'Is it bad, Mum?' she asked.

'She should be all right now they've taken her in. If there's anything troubles them they'll get the baby started early so's to bring the blood pressure down.'

'She'll be all right, won't she?'

'Of course she will. Dozens of women have blood pressure at the end of their time, and none the worse once it's over,' Mrs Earnshaw said.

'You sure about that, Mum?' Trevor said.

'Mrs French round the corner was in hospital four months with blood pressure before the twins were born, and look at her now.'

'I don't want Jeannie to get like Mrs French.'

'I didn't say they had to weigh half a ton after.'

'The doctor said it was common enough,' Trevor said.

'Did he say how long he was keeping her in?'

'Only a day or two, if it gets better. If it doesn't, she'll have to stay till the baby's come.'

'Why don't you sleep here till she's back with you again? You can have your room, there's only Dad's fishing gear to clear out.'

'I might do that.'

Helping her mother to make up the bed that hadn't been slept in since Trevor's marriage, Bee said again, 'Jean will be all right, won't she?'

'Have to go on what the doctor says.'

'And the baby? The baby'll be all right?'

'There's always a risk, even when everything goes straightforward, and blood pressure's what I don't like to hear about. But I don't want to say anything to Trev, he's worried enough as it is. There's nothing any of us can do, anyway, only wait and see.'

'First Thursday and now this. I feel as if I'd been waiting to see what happens for years.'

'You learn to live with it,' her mother said.

The next day was bad. Trevor came back miserable from the hospital, where he'd been told that Jean had got to stay in for the present. Bee, rehearsing all the time in her mind what she would say to Thursday, wondering what the doctor would ask her, found that she resented the sight of Trevor's anxiety, as if it actually added to her own. She was ashamed of her feelings, but she couldn't get rid of them. It was as if she wanted the right to be the only person in the family with anything to worry about.

Sunday was fine. Mr Tenterden arrived early in an old black Morris, with Miss Codell sitting beside him. When Bee had got into the back, with the picnic lunch in a carrier bag beside her, he said, 'I hope you don't mind, Miss Codell's coming with us. We'd planned to go out for the day anyhow, so I thought we could all have a breath of country air together.'

'I shan't come into the hospital. I shall go for a walk outside and enjoy the sun,' Miss Codell said.

'It's rather pretty country round there. Hills and plenty of trees. And the river, of course,' Mr Tenterden said.

'What's in your bag, Bee? Something for Thursday?'

'My mother's made us a picnic. There'll be plenty. She said we'd better have enough in case Thursday came out with us.'

'I don't know if they'd let him do that. But how kind of your mother!'

'Anyway I'm sure there'll be enough.'

They didn't talk much on the way. The two in front occasionally spoke to each other, but most of Mr Tenterden's attention was needed by the road, which was jammed with other cars trying to get out of the city as quickly as possible. Bee was grateful for the silence. Although she couldn't think consecutively of what was coming, couldn't plan, couldn't imagine what the hospital, or the doctor, or even what Thursday might be like, she didn't want to be interrupted. Her thoughts went round and round in her head; they never got anywhere.

As they got further out of London she began to notice the country. It was a long time since she'd seen it, she'd forgotten what it looked like in full summer. Last year she'd spent two weeks in France, where it had been dusty and hot and bleached. The year before that they'd all been to the sea in August. Bee wondered if she'd ever seen anything quite like this before: so green, so pink and rosy in the hedges, the occasional acid yellow of a mustard field: everything quite still, even the great trees standing unstirred by any breeze, as if they were asleep in the daytime, Bee thought. 'Going to be hot,' Mr Tenterden said from the front. 'It's almost midsummer,' Miss Codell said softly. Bee didn't speak. She was lost in the dreaming countryside, spread around her as the trees spread their huge branches full of hardly whispering leaves.

The hospital was a sprawling collection of buildings of yellow brick and grey stone. Ugly, surrounded by a high wall. Mr Tenterden asked at the entrance gates for Dr Petrie, and they were directed to the main block, standing in the centre of the grounds. They drove past flower beds full of roses, the stems of the little standard trees rather thin and stiff below, but with heads heavy with colour. Their scent filled the air, and Bee felt dizzy, partly with their sweetness, mostly with her fear. There were people sitting in chairs on the grass and on benches on the gravel paths. Bee wondered if they were patients. They looked quite ordinary, they wore ordinary clothes, there wasn't anything she could have named about their behaviour that you could call odd. Perhaps it was because these were hospital grounds and she was expecting to see patients with mental disturbances that she felt something was different about them. It wasn't until they had reached the main block and she was getting out of the car, that she realized what the something was. All those people, sitting, standing, walking, had been alone. No one had been speaking to any-one else. 'Is it the separateness that makes them mad?' Bee wondered. Is madness being alone in your own country? Not talking the same language as anyone else? If just one man got left alone for years on the moon, would he be mad?

They waited in a little office. Not like a hospital room except for its white walls. It had a carpet, pictures, bright curtains, two comfortable chairs. Mr Tenterden said, 'I'm not going to stay with you when Dr Petrie comes, Bee. I think you'll get on better with him by yourself. Miss Codell and I will be around somewhere outside.'

Bee nodded. It was all right for them, there were two of them, they'd be together. Whatever she had come to do, she had to do alone.

Dr Petrie came in. He was a small, youngish man, fair-haired with glasses. He shook hands all round, listened to Mr Tenterden's explanations and then saw him and Miss Codell out. He shut the door behind them, motioned Bee into one of the easy chairs and sat down himself in the other.

'Would you mind if I ask you a few questions?'

Bee shook her head.

'Or would you rather just talk? Tell me anything you think I ought to know?'

Bee shook her head again. She felt wound up, like a spring that has been coiled too tightly. If it sprang open suddenly she would burst into tears. Ridiculous, there was nothing yet to upset her. If she opened her mouth to talk, all that would come out would be a sharp cry, a protest against the pain. She kept her mouth shut.

'Have you known this boy for long?' Dr Petrie asked.

'Four years,' Bee muttered.

'You've known him very well, have you?'

'Quite well,' Bee said reluctantly.

'Better than anyone else has, do you think?'

'I don't know.' She did know, but she couldn't make herself say it.

'Let's say you know him very well. What sort of person would you say he was? Easy to get to know, or not?'

'Not,' Bee said.

'Did he have many friends that you knew of?'

'No.'

'But he did have some? You weren't the only one?'

'No.'

'These friends. Were they mostly boys or girls?'

'I don't know.'

'Perhaps you were his only girl friend. Were you?'

'I don't know.'

The young doctor sighed, and Bee could see why. She wasn't being helpful at all. She must seem to him either terribly stupid or very unwilling to tell him anything. It was awful. The trouble was that the questions he was asking were questions which couldn't be answered in two words, which was all she had to give.

There was a pause after the sigh. Then the doctor began again.

'Is he an intelligent boy? Did he do well at school?'

'Yes.'

'Did people like him? Or did they think him a bit odd?'

'They liked him. But they thought he was different too.'

'Try to explain, won't you? How was he different?' The doctor sounded encouraged for the first time in the interview.

Bee struggled. 'I don't know.'

She could hear that she'd been disappointing again in the tone of the doctor's voice as he asked the next question.

'Tell me, do you think he's changed at all since you've known him?'

There was a silence.

'I'm sorry,' Bee said.

'Sorry for what?'

'I don't seem able to say anything you want.'

'You're embarrassed perhaps, talking to a stranger about your private affairs?'

'It's not that.'

'What then?'

But Bee couldn't explain that somehow not only her answers, but his questions too were wrong. This doctor was thinking of someone who didn't exist, a patient whose name happened to be Thursday. It was like trying to explain how someone smelled and felt to a stranger who only knew his face from a photograph. Or who had never seen him alive, had only looked at him after death.

The doctor sighed again.

'Try to tell me about the change you noticed in him.'

Bee's ear heard again that cold voice saying, 'Leave me alone. I just want to be left alone.'

'He didn't want me,' she managed to say.

'And he had before?'

She nodded. 'You look ugly when you cry,' he had said. She wouldn't cry. She wouldn't, wouldn't cry.

'What do you mean by want?' the doctor asked.

Bee, surprised, said, more easily than she'd spoken before, 'You know. Want me.'

'Want in what sense?' the doctor said.

Bee felt something different in his tone. She felt as if he were suggesting something to her, waiting for her to make an expected answer. He reminded her of dogs she'd seen sniffing the air, excited, on the track of something they recognized and in a moment would be after. She said, slowly, 'He liked me.'

'Liked to be with you?'

'Yes.'

174

'Did he want you in a physical sense?'

Bee stared.

'Sex. Did he want to have sexual relations with you?' the young doctor said rather quickly, as if he wanted to get the question out and over.

'No.'

'You didn't? You were his girl friend, weren't you?' the doctor said.

'It wasn't like that.'

'Suppose you tell me how it was, then?'

He was trying to help. He waited for her to say something. Bee would have liked to be able to talk, just to talk without stopping to think, without bothering whether she said the right thing, whether she was understood or not. It would have meant bursting out with tears as well as with words, it would have been the unloosening of everything that was dammed up inside her, it would have been a tidal wave of misery and speech and love.

She couldn't. She was locked in silence. If the doctor could only have said the right word, touched the right chord, she might have been released. If he had seemed to be talking of a person, not a cipher, if he had spoken to her direct, human to human, if he had been older – or perhaps younger – if he'd spoken of Thursday by name, if he'd spoken of him with liking, or even with dislike or hate, she might have been able to respond. But the conversation, like the white walls of the room, was impersonal and sterile. Bee saw suddenly that the comfortable chairs and the carpet and the picture were brave attempts to make this place something more than an institutional background; they were an offer of friendship, of humanity. And it might have worked. If the doctor could have talked as if he were an ordinary young man; if Bee had felt that anything she said might provoke a normal human reaction, that he'd be

175

surprised or shocked or irritated, she might have been able to accept the offer to talk. But the fact that he was obviously determined to understand everything, to be infinitely tolerant and impossibly broadminded, made the whole attempt at a conversation unreal. Bee was silent.

'There's nothing so shocking about sex, you know. To have sexual desires is very natural at your age. I'm sure you know that,' Dr Petrie said, almost as if he were encouraging himself rather than Bee.

'I know,' Bee said.

'Perhaps you were surprised when he first made sexual advances to you. You may have frightened him by giving the impression of being more outraged than you actually felt,' Dr Petrie suggested.

'It's never been like that,' Bee said.

'Perhaps you don't think people ought to have sex before marriage?' Dr Petrie said, as if he had discovered some out-of-the-way opinion, like thinking the Stuarts should still be on the English throne or not holding with taking aspirin when you had a headache.

'I don't know.'

'Your parents are fairly permissive, are they?'

'I don't know.'

'Well, are they or aren't they?' the doctor said, a little impatient at last.

Bee said, 'I don't know,' again. And again she felt how little these questions had to do with real people or ordinary life. Like people in books of mathematical problems who filled leaking tanks, or drove certain distances at x miles per hour, or who had two and a half children per household, the people the doctor was speaking about weren't people she knew. Believing in sex before marriage – or not believing – had nothing to do with what she was feeling now about Thursday. And 'permissive' meant nothing if it was used to describe her mother. These words were tags, labels, headlines in newspapers and chapter names in books, not words for describing how you felt about people, live, breathing people, who said one thing one day and another the next, who saw what might be the sensible thing to do but didn't always do it, who made rules and then understood if you had to break them. How could you contain a whole extraordinary person in a couple of words in a catalogue?

She realized that while she'd thought all this, Dr Petrie must have been talking to her. She caught the end of a question. '. . . a satisfactory relationship?' She looked at him blankly, then fell back on the only safe answer. She said, 'I don't know' again.

'Isn't there anything you'd like to tell me?' the doctor said, and Bee could hear a sort of winding-up despair in his voice.

'No.'

There was a pause.

'That's all you can say?'

Bee nodded. There was another pause.

'We'd better see if we can find your friends,' Dr Petrie said, getting up and opening the door.

'Please . . .' Bee said quickly, and the doctor turned towards her hopefully.

'I may see Thursday, mayn't I?'

'I'll just find out where he's likely to be,' the doctor said. He picked up the telephone receiver and dialled a number. Bee heard him say, 'The boy Townsend . . .', and she felt again the impersonality, the remoteness of this institutionalized place. 'He's out in the garden apparently. We'll go and find him,' Dr Petrie said, leading the way out of the office and not looking back to see if she were following. Bee knew he was fed up with her and wanted to get rid of her as soon as possible. She couldn't blame him. It wasn't his fault that she hadn't been able to say anything that could help.

CHAPTER EIGHTEEN

THURSDAY sat on a curved stone bench in the middle of a
rose garden. All around, the blooms were deep crimson and
glowing gold, orange shot with yellow like a sunset sky in
summer, china pink. The scent was heady. You thought
you'd got accustomed to it, that you wouldn't notice it any
more, and then suddenly it hit you, a fresh wave of sweetness on the air, almost like something you could put out
your hand and touch. Honey bees murmured their satisfac-
tion and excitement, pushing their way into the open-faced,
flushed flowers for nectar. All around, the great trees stood
watching, their leaves hardly moving, drowsing in the midday sun. If the Sleeping Beauty could have pricked her
finger on the spindle out of doors, Bee thought, it would
have been in a place like this, a stone circle within this
enchanted, scented garden. No one else was there. She and
Thursday sat facing each other across the sundial at the
centre of the small circle of benches. The insects hummed
and the leaves quivered, the sun was directly overhead, and
everything waited, half asleep, for what would happen.

Against the colour and the sweetness, Thursday looked
strange. When Bee had seen him last he had at least walked
and spoken, he had had some impulse inside himself to
action, however contrary an impulse it had been. Now he
had nothing. He sat almost quite still; he looked at Bee and
he looked at the roses, but his expression didn't change. In
this theatre of colour and light, he was grey and withdrawn
and cold.

'Thursday?' Bee said.

He didn't speak.

'Do you know who I am?'

179

His eyes flickered over her indifferently and he didn't answer. This wouldn't do. She must try something else.

'I've come to see you.'

He looked past her, at the flowers.

'I've come a long way.'

His eyes didn't move.

'I've come from London. Mr Tenterden brought me in his car.'

She felt the slackening of his interest.

'I've come because I wanted to see you.'

That was better.

'I know what's happened to you. I've come because I want to help.'

There was a change in his attitude, so slight anyone might have missed it. Bee didn't.

'Old Mrs Smith told me. I didn't understand when I saw you before.'

He said, very slowly, 'Mrs Smith.'

'In the newspaper shop. Old Mrs Smith. You know.'

He repeated in the same quiet voice, 'Old Mrs Smith.'

'She told me how to help you.'

Suddenly, shockingly, he cried out with a loud voice, 'No one can help me!' Faces beyond the rosebuds turned towards them. A man in a short white coat started to walk in their direction, then stopped and stood waiting to see what would happen next. Thursday was trembling. After a moment or two he stopped. It was somehow more frightening to see him suddenly become quiet and still.

'Don't the doctors help?' Bee asked.

No answer.

'Are they nice here? Are they kind to you?'

Silence.

'What does it feel like? What are you thinking? Thursday. Can't you tell me?'

He continued to look, immovably, at the ground.

'I saw the psychiatrist just now. Do you talk to him? Or anyone?'

Still that stony silence.

'Are they going to give you electric shocks?'

She might as well not have spoken. He gave no sign of having heard.

'It's the nineteenth of June today,' Bee said.

He didn't look at her.

'In another four days it'll be the twenty-third.'

No sign.

'That's Midsummer's Eve.'

He didn't move.

'Thursday!' Bee said urgently.

At the sound of his name, he lifted his head. His eyes were empty, but at least he was looking at her.

'Thursday. On Midsummer's Eve . . .'

She stopped, feeling a fool. What had Midsummer's Eve to do with psychiatrists and hospitals, or with nervous breakdowns, or science, or the way people lived now, the sort of things they believed in? But he was still looking at her, and she went on.

'She says that's the time it'd be easiest.'

He stared straight at her with unblinking eyes.

'I can do it, Thursday. I know I can. If you'll only believe . . .'

His stony face believed nothing.

'I know it sounds like nonsense. But when she said it, it seemed as if she really knew.'

No movement.

'She said she'd seen it happen to other people. Just like you. Sort of not really being here.'

'Not being here,' Thursday said, very slow, as if the words were being invented for the first time inside him.

'Part of you isn't here. They've taken you away.'

'They?'

'I don't want to say the name.'

Now his eyes were attentive to her words.

'I've got to get you back. Thursday! I must!'

He didn't answer that.

'Somehow. On Midsummer's Eve. Thursday, you've got to be there!'

'There?'

'I don't know.' Bee was confused. She had spoken without thinking. She saw his eyes begin to cloud over, she felt his interest wane. She cried out, 'Thursday!', caught his momentary consciousness of her in his eyes, and said, without stopping to think, 'Our place!' Directly she heard her own words she knew that this was right. It had been from there he'd been taken, it would be there he would come back to. She asked, 'How will you get there? It's a long way from here.'

'A long way,' he repeated.

'Will they let you out,'

'I shall never get out,' he said, desolately. His face shut down again, he wasn't looking at Bee now, his vision was turned only inward.

'I can't come back here,' Bee said. Even if she could have got here it wouldn't be any good. Although you might think that if such a thing as magic existed, it must be in the country, how could there be anything so mysterious, so unscientific, in a hygienic, planned, tidy place like this? 'How will you get away?' she asked Thursday again, but he was beyond communication and turned on her only the blank look she dreaded.

'You must come there,' she said again. But he gave no sign of hearing.

Someone laid a hand on her arm. It was Miss Codell,

with Mr Tenterden behind her. The man in the short white coat was there too. He came forward and spoke to Thursday kindly but meaninglessly, as one speaks to an animal or a very young child. Bee watched, aching: Thursday didn't answer, seemed not to have heard or noticed that he'd been addressed. The man put a gentle but firm arm over his shoulders and turned him towards the hospital buildings. Bee's ache didn't become less when she saw Thursday walk obediently away from her without once looking back.

CHAPTER NINETEEN

> 'Tomorrow night when Phoebe doth behold
> Her silver visage in the watery glass,
> Decking with liquid pearl the bladed grass,
> (A time that lovers' flights doth still conceal,)
> Through Athens' gates have we devised to steal.'

There was a noticeable pause.
'Bee! Bee! Wake up! Your cue!'
'I'm sorry,' Bee said.
'That's the third time you've missed it,' Alison said.
'I'm terribly sorry. Give it to me again.'
'Through Athens' gates have we devised to steal,' Timmy
Spender said, sing-song, deliberately making nonsense of it.

> 'And in the wood, where often you and I
> Upon faint primrose beds were wont to lie,
> Emptying our bosoms of their counsels sweet,
> There my Lysander and myself shall meet:
> And thence from Athens turn away our eyes,
> To seek new friends and stranger companies . . .'

She'd learned it quickly after all: finding it not difficult
because it was suddenly alive with meaning. How could she
ever have thought it was boring or childish? It might have
been written for her. When she read the poetry to herself
she *was* Hermia. 'Am I not Hermia? Are you not Lysander? I am as fair now as I was erstwhile, Since night you
loved me: yet since night you left me . . .' Faced with
Timmy, who was short and solid, with tow-coloured hair
and sandy lashes, and who could spring suddenly to great-
ness and act superbly when he had an audience, but who

went through rehearsals without showing a spark of under-standing or dramatic sense, she was apt to get lost, think-ing, instead of listening for her cues. By this time she knew nearly the whole play by heart; and often, as had happened now, she had heard the verse, the questions and answers, the protestations, the harangues, the vows, the arguments played out in the vaulted theatre of her skull, so that she hardly knew who was really speaking, or even whether the lines had been spoken aloud or not.

'Don't go,' Alison said sharply.

'Why not? I don't come on again for ages.'

'Honestly, Bee! Don't you ever listen to anything? We're not doing it straight through, we're just doing the lovers and Oberon and Puck.'

The rehearsal dragged on. Bee tried to attend, tried to feel, in the crowded, chalky classroom, the desolation she knew from her own experience. But it wouldn't do. She said the words woodenly, as far from real feeling as Timmy was. It all sounded stupid, unmeaning, like an old-fashioned, out-dated play acted by school-children. No wonder she kept on missing cues. The only people who spoke the words as if they meant them were Marigold and Peter Dinsley. They spoke to each other about the magic herb which changed the eyes of the lovers, as if it were a part of everyday life. Magic was not strange to them. For the period of the rehearsal it was the air they breathed. Mari-gold was good, she looked right for the part and spoke well, but Peter was inspired; when he was speaking he was not only a supernatural being. He was a king. It was his right to command. It was unthinkable that Titania would not give up the little Indian boy when he asked; and there was something more that Bee couldn't quite define. It wasn't exactly evil, it certainly wasn't goodness. What was it? What came into her head was the word 'power'. At the end of the afternoon, Lynne said to her, 'Peter's terrific. The rest of you aren't terribly good yet, but he's super.'

'We're all rotten except him,' Bee said.

'The lovers are soppy anyway. Even when I saw real actors doing it, I thought they were dead boring. But Peter's quite as good as their Oberon was. Better, in fact.'

'He sounds as if he meant it,' Bee said.

'He gives me a funny feeling. You know when he says that bit, "But we are spirits of another sort ..." I feel he kind of might do anything.'

'You mean he doesn't bother whether it's good or bad, he just goes ahead and does what he wants?' Bee said.

'That's right.'

'Perhaps that's how they really are.'

'Like who are?'

'Oberon. Puck. All of them.'

'Oh, the fairies. How do you mean, really are?'

Bee just prevented herself from saying, as old Mrs Smith had, 'don't say the name!' She said instead, 'I mean, if there were any, that's how they'd be.'

'How?'

'Not meaning to be good or bad. Just happening. Like weather. Or like the sea.'

'You're crazy,' Lynne said, affectionately.

'I'm not!' Bee said, remembering the hospital and those people separated by their private worlds of madness.

'Sometimes you are. Talking about fairies as if they were real.'

Part of Bee agreed. She'd have said the same a month ago. Now she wasn't sure what she believed. If what seemed real to her was unreal for Thursday, and if his ideas could become so different and seem so crazy to her, how did anyone know which side of truth was the real one? Were

fairies any crazier than the sort of thing psychologists believed in? If you told a person that they were suffering
from the effects of things that had happened to them before
they could remember, was that any wilder than telling
them they'd been bewitched?

'What's wrong?' Lynne asked.

'Nothing. Why?'

'I just thought. How's your brother's wife?'

Feeling guilty, because she hadn't been thinking about
Jean, Bee said, 'They're not going to let her home till she's
had the baby.'

'There's nothing wrong with that. Lots of people stay in
hospital for a bit before the baby comes.'

'I can see Mum's worried,' Bee said doubtfully.

'I am sorry, Bee. Awful for you. Hope she's better soon.'

Too much was happening too quickly. Yet the days
seemed endless, as if the time she was waiting for would
never come. It was hot and humid. The city sweated under
a ceiling of low grey cloud, the air so heavy it felt like
breathing in saturated cotton wool. Headache weather.
Everyone seemed tired and short-tempered. The nights were
unbearably stuffy: the darkness thickened the atmosphere
without bringing any relief in a drop in temperature. Bee
felt as if she were living on the edge of something, she
didn't know what. At school the class above hers were taking exams, the people were irritable and touchy, and the
rest of the school suffered. It should have been a relief to
come home, but it wasn't. Trevor was in a state of restless
anxiety, couldn't sit still, couldn't settle to anything; if he
wasn't spending the evenings in the sitting-room with the
television on, staring unseeing at the big screen, he'd be
walking up and down the kitchen, where Mrs Earnshaw

generally was to be found, talking. Bee had never heard him talk so much, he'd always been a rather silent boy and young man. He talked at first about his most recent visit to the hospital, about what the doctor had said, what the ward sister had done, about the women in the neighbouring beds, about the meals and the nights and the temperature charts and the nurses. Then, later, he'd talk about Jean : not fluently and coherently, but in snatches, like, perhaps, the chorus of a song with many different verses. Bee, half trying to learn the products of Denmark, and the main trading ports of the Baltic, half listening to Trevor's talk, heard him again and again, at the end of each story of what they'd done together and what they'd planned, speak of what they'd do when Jean came home from hospital. 'We'll be going to the Motor Show in October. Jean's to help me choose a car,' Trevor said. 'We shan't go away this summer, Jean'll be a bit tied with the baby,' he said. 'We thought maybe we'd get over to Lincoln to see Jean's Mum's gran, and show her her great great grandson,' he said another time. At first Bee had been astonished and cheered, believing these statements meant that Jean wasn't any longer in danger. Then she realized that they weren't statements of fact, but of hope. Trevor needed to make them, they were a sort of lifeline. To all of them Mrs Earnshaw said no more than, 'That's right,' or 'Of course,' or 'You do that, lad.' She never questioned the probability of any of Trevor's schemes. It was, Bee thought, as if she was saying Amen to an often repeated prayer that appealed for the possibility of hope.

On Wednesday, however, there was news. When Bee got back from school she found her mother moving around the kitchen in an agitated, aimless way unlike her usual self.

'She's started,' Mrs Earnshaw said.

'Who? Started what?' Bee asked.

'Jean. She's in labour. Started dinner time. Trev was round here just now.'

'How is she?'

'Very good. Cheerful, Trev says. Can't wait for it to be over now. Nor can he, poor lad.'

'How long will it take?' Bee asked.

'Can't tell with the first. Might be tonight, might not be till tomorrow morning.'

'That long! That'd be *hours*!' Bee cried.

'Takes two days or more, sometimes. I just hope Jean's one of the lucky ones, that's all. Blood pressure's what I don't like. If it wasn't for that I wouldn't be worrying.'

'It's good she's in hospital, though, isn't it? I mean, they'll make sure she's all right, won't they?'

'They'll do their best,' Mrs Earnshaw said, but she sounded unconvinced. She continued preparations for the evening meal, but not in her usual calm way. To Bee it was unexpectedly disturbing to see her mother unable to concentrate. It made her realize the extent of the anxiety which hung over the family as nothing else could.

To begin with it wasn't too bad. She was even grateful that her mother's mind was occupied so that she didn't notice that Bee herself was on edge. But during the evening it got worse, she'd have given anything not to have this extra burden laid on her. After ten o'clock her father went out to telephone the hospital from the nearby callbox. Her mother sat with deliberate calm in front of the television, but Bee knew she wasn't seeing the screen. When she heard her husband's key in the lock she was in the passage immediately asking, 'What did they say?'

'No change, they said.'

'Did they say how she was?'

'Fairly comfortable, they said. For what that's worth.'

'Maybe they've given her an injection. Did you ask how long it's going to be?'

'They didn't know. That means not just yet, doesn't it, Mum?' Mr Earnshaw said.

'Mm. Where's Trev?'

'With Jean. Sister I spoke to said they'd be sending him home if it looked like nothing was going to happen tonight.'

'I'll make a cup of tea,' Mrs Earnshaw said. Before the kettle had boiled Trev came in, sat down at the kitchen table and put his head down on his arms.

'Is it that bad?' his mother asked.

'They say not to worry,' Trevor said slowly.

'Then ...?'

'It's the seeing her being hurt and not being able to do anything.'

'She having a lot of pain?'

'Comes and goes. Trouble is, when it goes you know it's going to last that much longer.'

'How's she keeping?'

Trev didn't answer. His head went back on to his arms again. Mrs Earnshaw poured out the tea and put a cup by him.

'Drink it up, lad. Then you'd best get some sleep. She'll be needing you tomorrow.'

Bee felt she oughtn't to look at Trevor. She hadn't seen him cry for years, not since she was a really little girl. Seeing him like that, his eyes red, his face wet and distorted, she saw him suddenly not as her brother, a familiar figure she never properly looked at, but as somebody outside herself and her family. A grown man. It made his misery larger, somehow, not just the unhappiness of someone she'd seen cry as a child. It gave her a shiver down her spine. She saw that Trev and Jean, who'd seemed so ordinary and safe in their happiness, could have everything suddenly taken away from them. She felt the narrowness of the ledge between the beginning of life and death. She saw her mother troubled, her father looking on with grave eyes. She felt unsafe, as if everything she had once been sure of might prove wrong. Girls like Jean shouldn't be allowed to lose their babies, shouldn't have to run the risk of dying. Boys like Thursday shouldn't become cold and distant, with hard stony faces as if they'd been visited by a Gorgon head. She wanted to cry out the question, 'Is nothing safe?' But no one in the kitchen could have given her the reassurance she wanted. What she was looking at was three other people who had felt the ground beneath them shake and split into deep and dangerous crevices, just as she had herself.

The next morning, when Bee came down to breakfast, after a restless night of uncomfortable, half-remembered dreams, she found her mother clearing the remains of Trev's meal. He hadn't eaten much by the look of it.

'Did they send for him from the hospital?' she asked.

'Not a word. Dad went with him and came back to tell me what was going on.'

'What?'

'Nothing new. Jean's just the same.'

'She can't go on much longer. I mean, can she?'

'They'll be keeping a watch on her.'

'Mum!' Bee said, and stopped.

'What?'

'I wish you'd tell me.'

'Tell you what?'

'If it's. You know. Dangerous. I mean. Do people ever? I mean, could a person die?'

'Could be.'

191

'I thought nowadays they could prevent it. I thought having babies was safe now.'

'Things can go wrong even nowadays.'

'Could that happen? To Jean?'

'More likely they'd have to let the baby go.'

'They couldn't!' Bee cried.

'If it was Jean or the baby, Bee?'

'I suppose so. You shouldn't have to choose.'

'Hope they don't.'

'When d'you think we'll know?'

'Any time now. You'd best be getting to school, Bee. No reason for you to be late, whatever the day.'

But it wasn't just any ordinary day. It was Midsummer's Eve, the day before the night when something out of the ordinary was going to happen. It was the day when Jean might have her baby. It was the day when Jean and Trev's baby might die. It was the day when Thursday must some-how escape from his prison. Bee went to school in a sort of dream. She felt as if her head didn't belong to her, as if her feet were sinking inches deep into the pavement instead of touching hard stone, as if what she saw and what she heard had nothing to do with her. Her eyes and her ears took note, but weren't sending the proper sort of message to her brain. At any moment they might start to send strange messages, crazy messages about things other people couldn't see or hear, as if the outside skin of the ordinary world might suddenly be peeled off, showing her – and only her – a quite different, frightening world underneath. The atmosphere was like it is before a thunderstorm; the noises in the street had strange echoes, the light had purplish shadows behind it. Bee had felt like this when she was fever-ish. Nothing was ordinary. Everything was strange.

There was no one at home when she rushed back, against all school rules, in the lunch hour. No one was there. Bee imagined her mother called to the hospital for a deathbed scene, before she remembered that it was the afternoon when Mrs Earnshaw went to a meeting of what Bee's father called the Old Girls. Bee didn't know quite what the old girls did – visited old people? Looked after babies? Helped people to find new homes? Or just talked and drank tea? The house was painfully empty, the cooker cold and the rooms unwelcoming. Bee meant to help herself to a bar of cooking chocolate, but when she opened the cupboard she quite suddenly didn't want it. She shut the cupboard and left. No Mum, no Jean. It was mockery of normal life.

It was a hideous afternoon and it lasted for ever. Bee didn't know what lessons she sat through, didn't hear anything that was said. She felt so odd she began to wonder if she really was going to be ill. 'Bee! Bee! What's the matter with you? I've been trying to make you hear for the last ten minutes,' Lynne said.

'Sorry.'

'You look funny, Bee. Do you feel all right?'

'I don't know.'

'Shall I take you to the sick room?'

'No. Thanks.'

'You sure? You're all white and sweating. Don't you think you ought?'

'It's only another hour till four o'clock. I'll be all right.'

She was, but only just. In spite of being in a hurry to get back, she had to let the rest of the school leave before her. She couldn't face a crowd, the noise and stuffiness of the downstairs cloakrooms, the endless questions about her appearance. Antonia Codell found her wandering about the passage outside the wash-rooms. Like Lynne, she asked, 'Are you all right?'

'I'm just going home,' Bee said quickly.

'Sure you're fit to go alone? You look very tired.'

'I'll be all right, thank you,' Bee said.

'Bee,' Miss Codell said, hesitating.

'Yes?'

'Don't be too unhappy about Thursday. I'm sure he will get better. Doctors can't tell everything, you know.'

'What did they say?'

'Nothing much. Brian did ask, but they wouldn't commit themselves.'

'It was awful. I couldn't make him understand.'

'But he will! He will understand! We'll go and visit him again, and soon he'll know how you feel,' the girl said, almost singing her conviction, so that Bee looked at her, astonished, then saw that it wasn't Bee's feelings she was talking about, it was her own. For a moment Bee forgot Thursday, forgot Jean, forgot her heavy eyes and fogged brain. She shared the joy of acknowledged love. She said, 'Mr Tenterden?' and saw on Antonia's lips a dreaming, half-secret, tender smile. A moment later a telephone rang and she'd gone. Bee got her things out of the deserted cloak-room and left.

Her mother had been watching for her and came out on to the pavement.

'Jean?' Bee asked, dry-mouthed.

'Nothing different. Trev's asleep. He got back just now and before I could make him a cup of tea he'd dropped off. That's what I came out to say, don't make a noise.'

Bee pussy-footed along the passage. Looking in through the sitting-room door, she saw Trevor, spread in the atti-tude of exhaustion over one of the chairs. In the kitchen with the door shut, Mrs Earnshaw said, 'He's to be back at the hospital at nine. He may as well get some sleep now.'

'What's happening at nine?'

'Nothing's likely to happen before then, that's all.'

'I didn't know it could take so long,' Bee said.

'First generally takes the longest,' Mrs Earnshaw said.

'Why?'

'Most things get easier when you've had a bit of practice. Cup of tea?'

'I'm too hot. I'll just have a drink of water.'

'What're you doing this evening?'

'I've got some work. Why?' Bee asked, startled.

'Dad and I might go round to the hospital with Trev. You all right here on your own?'

'I'll be all right,' Bee said, wishing it wasn't Jean's trouble that was going to make things easier for her.

'Anyone you'd like to ask round? I didn't cook, but there's cold meat and salad.'

'I might. Don't worry about me, Mum. I'll be all right.'

She went upstairs feeling bad. She might get back home before her parents; if she didn't there would be a row, and she'd have nothing to say in her own defence. She'd often done what she'd been told not to before, of course, but never anything like this. She wondered if she could possibly go through with it. So many things could go wrong. She didn't even know if Thursday would come. She might wait there, alone, for hours and for nothing. Her guts slithered inside her, and her knees felt weak. She went into her bedroom and spread the books out on the table she used as a desk, but she knew she wouldn't be able to work. She heard her mother moving about quietly downstairs, and she thought of Trevor, wearily asleep, and of Jean in a long, dangerous labour. Everyone was waiting for something to happen tonight. It was like a piece of music where, even if you hadn't heard it before, you knew it was building up towards the end, that there'd be a great crash of chords with all the instruments playing at once, saying something that might be joyful or might be sad, but which would anyway be important. That would make sense of everything that had gone before. But sometimes it was difficult to wait, you got tired or you got anxious and impatient. You got frightened. Bee was all these things. And because it was midsummer the day seemed endless, the light stretched the evening into infinity. Bee felt that darkness would never come.

CHAPTER TWENTY

IT was more than half dark when Bee reached the bomb site, a heavy evening, purple and grey, the overcast sky pressing down on top of the city, shutting it into breathless darkness for the night. Buildings loomed over the streets as if threatening to fall and crush passers-by beneath their weight. As Bee turned into Farmer's Lane, a goods train, one of the very few left on that stretch of line, jangled slowly across the track above her. The deserted factory building was as gaunt as a gibbet. Bee looked up and down the lane, saw that it was empty, and squeezed through the gap in the hoarding wall.

On the other side it was even darker. Farmer's Lane was not well lit, and the hoarding was just high enough to shield the bomb site from the feeble illumination of the street lamps. Bee climbed into a colourless world. The grass, the willow herb, the brambles, the spindly flowers of the cow-parsley were all grey around her, waist-high and still. The mound in the corner, and the steps that led down to the arched passage-way were shadowy black. Above and to her left, the house wall caught the light from the street and glimmered a ghostly greenish white, the irregularities standing out horribly, like wounds.

The rattle of the goods train died away. It was very quiet.

Bee pushed her way cautiously to the steps and sat on them. From here she could see the gap in the hoarding, but, with the dark arch behind her, she wasn't too visible herself. She wanted to be able to keep watch without being watched.

As soon as she had stopped moving she became aware that the silence and stillness around her were not absolute. The grass round her ankles and knees rustled with her breath; a mosquito sang its high warning siren in her ear, and she swiped to keep it away. Two swallows chased each other round the tall factory building above her, silent except for the beat of their wings and the swift turn of their bodies against the heavy air. From somewhere on her right a late wandering bee buzzed angrily at a closing flower. Right up by the factory roof she could see a bat, flittering in a very fast swooping flight. Further away she heard the hooting of a car horn, the screech of brakes, and behind all these small single noises was the hum of the city's traffic, impersonal, huge, anonymous, perpetual. As far as Bee knew it never stopped. Even if you woke in the middle of the night you always heard it. It became part of your life, like the tick of the clock in your room, like your mother's voice; like your heart beat.

The sky overhead took on a curious sultry reddish glow. It reflected the light of the city. Bee wondered, as she often had before, why the reflection was always red or orange, when the lights themselves were mostly yellow or white. The colour spread like a theatrical effect. It was already much darker. Bee could only just see the glimmer of her own bare arms. She wished suddenly that she had brought a torch.

Something moved near her. For a moment her pulses stopped beating, then hammered so that they hurt. She heard the movements again, stealthy, persistent, quite close. She sat as still as death. She could just see the disturbance of the tall grass ten feet away from her, like a ripple coming nearer. Then an elegant cat shape stepped out on to the brickwork of the steps where she sat. It stopped for a moment and the gleaming green eyes regarded her, then it walked on, silent and solitary, and disappeared again into the long vegetation. Bee could just hear the rustle of dry stalks as it moved away from her. It had been silly to be frightened of a cat. She ought to have known what it might be, she'd often seen cats here before. But of course never at night.

She wondered if it had been a black cat. That might have been lucky. It had been too dark to see. 'All cats are grey in the dark' came out of the part of her brain which stored old sayings, quotations, all sorts of odd things she must have heard somewhere, some time. She wasn't sure what this one was supposed to mean, but it was true. In this summer night everything, not only cats, was grey.

She shivered. Not because it was cold, it was still heavy and hot. The shiver was for the relief when the sight of the cat lifted the fear she'd felt while she could still only hear it.

She wondered how long she'd have to wait. She looked for her wristwatch, but it was already too dark to see. If its hands had been phosphorescent like the cat's eyes, she could have told the time. She thought that it would have been useful if the cat's eyes had actually given off light so that one could read a watch by them, like lamps. If another cat came past she might try holding her watch in the glow of its eyes.

As if in answer to her thoughts, a clock somewhere a long way away chimed a half-hour. Bee reckoned it must be half past ten. She had left her home as late as she dared, but she'd been too anxious to be off before her mother came back from the hospital to wait for long. Another hour and a half to midnight.

She thought at first that it was going to be intolerable. She thought that every unexpected sound would make her skin prickle and her heart stop. She thought that when the darkness was complete she would be as much lost as if she'd been in a jungle. She thought that the time she had to wait would seem an eternity. She thought that Thursday surely wouldn't come.

After the first quarter of an hour a sort of quietness settled on her. The great distant roar beyond the walls of her enclosure became a droning background, against which the little noises close to her were intimate, almost friendly. The warm air smelled of clover, of crushed grass and, less pleasantly, of petrol and soot. The suffused sky above continued to give just enough light to ensure that her now accustomed eyes made out the shapes surrounding her. Sitting on the lowest step, and leaning against another, she was not uncomfortable. From a long way off came the sound of separated notes played on some wind instrument, a thin trickle of a tune, reedy and plaintive. A radio, from a distant open window, Bee supposed. The notes pierced the heavy air like pinpoints of light through a mist, almost too widely separated to add up to a melody. The clock struck the three-quarters. It seemed very soon afterwards that it called the hour.

Bee heard it, and wondered what her mother was thinking. If she'd come home she'd be surprised and inclined to be cross; eleven o'clock was as late as Bee was supposed to stay out on a weekday night. But she wouldn't begin yet to be alarmed. And she might well not have got back herself yet. It all depended on Jean. Bee thought quickly and guiltily of Jean. For the last half-hour she'd forgotten her. She didn't want to imagine Jean as the principal actor in the film she'd seen at school, which had showed, more or less, the process of birth. She remembered the wide-eyed, childish look of the girl in the film as she did the pre-natal exercises and regularly visited the clinic for checkups. She remembered a body thrashing on a bed, a nurse's voice saying, 'Now then, Mrs Steadman.' She remembered the face of the same girl, turned sideways on a pillow, eyes wide again, mouth squared in fright and pain, and the camera then cutting to the other end of the bed; a group of the doctor, nurses, anonymous in surgical masks and caps, and the extraordinary sight of birth. Bee would never forget the look of the mother as she first saw her baby. A face made ugly by tears and pain and yet alive with joy. Something that had hurt that much, cost so much, was welcomed and loved.

She didn't know what was happening to Jean. For all she knew Jean might have died. It was odd how one could think about death without actually feeling anything. Saying to oneself, 'Jean may die,' and following the thought to its conclusion, leaving feeling out. Then suddenly the feeling side of it overcame her, and she saw what it would be like to have Jean gone, out of reach. No longer Jean, no unexpected responses, no warmth, no reality, nothing but saying 'Do you remember how she was?', something evoked, not living. It struck her suddenly sitting there in the suffused dim light of the reflected brightness in the sky, that she had never known till now what it might mean to lose somebody through death. She had never known what it was to have no hope. She had never been completely alone before.

It was the quickened beat of her own heart that told her what she had heard, before her slower brain had interpreted the message from her ears. When, suddenly, painfully awake, she listened, there was a new rhythm against the hum of the traffic and the sigh of the wind. Footsteps on a road, at a little distance, footsteps sounding hollow, somehow over-emphatic in this curiously apprehensive atmosphere; footsteps which approached the lane with apparent determination; footsteps which suddenly, for no apparent reason, hesitated, broke the sound pattern with an unexpected pause.

On her feet, her heart pounding, Bee said, 'Thursday!' She said it out loud, though there was no possibility of his hearing. The footsteps hadn't delayed again, they were coming nearer. Bee, cold and trembling, heard them stop the other side of the hoarding. There was a silence which she could interpret. Someone was climbing through the gap. Then the rustling of the long grass. With eyes now adapted to the night, she saw the figure approaching her. She moved, and knew by his jerking stop that he had seen her. In the emptiness of that ruined place, she and Thursday confronted each other.

'You got away,' she said.

He didn't speak. She could just make out that he stood in front of her with his hands dangling at his sides, his head down. She couldn't see his face, his expression. She didn't know if he was looking at her or not; but something about the unnatural quietness of his body made her say, abruptly, 'Thursday!'

If he turned his eyes towards her, it was too dark for her to see.

'I've been waiting for you,' Bee said.

'Waiting,' he repeated.

'I said I'd be here tonight.'

Silence.

'How did you get here from the hospital?' she asked.

'The hospital.'

'How did you get out? Did anyone see you leaving? Didn't they try to stop you?'

'They didn't see me leaving.'

'How did you get here? Did you take a train?'

No answer.

'You can't have walked! It's much too far,' Bee said.

'It's too far,' he repeated.

She couldn't imagine how he had done it, and it was clear he wasn't going to be able to explain. Part of Bee, an impatient, busy, active part, wanted to shake his story out of him; wanted to make him tell her how he'd got there, what he remembered, why he'd come. Another part, a bewildered, childish part, made her want to put the responsibility on him, to give up, to take his hand and lead him out of this place of shadows and whisperings, back to the streetlights and home and sanity. It was these two parts which made her ask him, 'What was it like in the hospital, Thursday? What did you think about while you were there?' And it was these that made her, when he didn't answer, just stood before her, dumb and silent, long to shake him, to call out, to run away, to hit him, anything so that there should be something happening, so that she wouldn't have to stay there waiting, her questions unanswered, not knowing whether he heard her, whether he knew she was there, a person and yet not a person. Old Mrs Smith's words came back to her, 'An image. A stock. Made of their stuff, the creature without the blessed soul.'

The clock struck the half-hour. In another thirty minutes it would be midnight.

Bee made another attempt at cold sense.

'Did the doctor know you were coming?'

The answer was terrifying. Thursday put back his head and cried out, aloud. He didn't mouth any words, he howled, like an animal in pain. Let out on the breathless night air, the sound trembling up into that heavy, close sky, it was horrible. Bee felt she had never heard pure misery before, but it was the misery of a being who had no language, it was unexplained. It was nothing but feeling. She knew then that talking was no good. Asking questions was no good. All she could do for Thursday now, as Mrs Smith had said, was to be with him.

She said, 'Thursday.'

He lowered his head. She saw in the dim light, the whites of his eyes, and knew he was looking towards her.

'It's all right. I know.'

He didn't move.

'I know what's wrong. I know about you not really being here.'

A quality in his attitude told her that she had his attention.

'I know about what happened. I know they took you away.'

He groaned, rather than said, 'Yes.'

'Thursday. It's Midsummer's Eve.'

He was listening intently.

'It's the night. It's the one night in the year.'

'The night,' he said.

'Thursday. I might be able to save you. She says I can. Mrs Smith says I can.'

He looked at her still, with those eyes that glinted in the dim light.

'Will you let me try?' She felt a fool. She didn't even know what she was asking to be allowed to do, and he didn't help her, he just stood.

'They'll try to keep you,' she said.

'They took me away,' he said.

'You remember that?' she asked, and he nodded.

'You want to come back?'

He stood for what seemed a long time without answering, then said very quietly, 'You?'

'I'd try. If I knew you wanted it.'

'I want it!' he said.

'Thursday. I don't know how.'

204

He didn't answer that.

'She said to hold you.'

'Hold me,' he said.

Bee stepped across the brickwork that separated them. For a moment she hesitated. He felt like a stranger. The Thursday she'd known would have given some sign. Then she remembered. This was and wasn't Thursday. She felt his strangeness as she'd never felt it before. As she put her arms around him, felt the boniness of his starved body, smelled the difference in his skin and his hair, she could have drawn back, could have called out that this wasn't the boy she'd known. But at least he stood still, he didn't shrink from her touch. It was his rigidity that was frightening. It was like embracing a stone figure, a statue. In that heated air even his skin was cold.

She said, 'Thursday.'

'Is that my name?' he asked her.

'It's what we've always called you,' she said.

'Is it my name?'

She said, boldly, 'Yes.' She would have given anything to be able to call him by another name, to have said, 'You are called Thomas,' any name which a boy of his age might have been given in love and pride. But she knew she mustn't lie. She said, 'Your name is Thursday.' She felt as if she were a priest baptizing a child for the first time.

'What does it mean?' he asked.

'It doesn't mean anything. It's just you.'

'Thursday?'

'Names can mean anything. It doesn't matter what it means.'

'I thought it was important, what it meant.'

'No.'

He clutched her suddenly. 'What's your name?'

'I'm Bee,' Bee said, shaken.

He said, 'Bee!' as if he'd never heard the name before. Still holding her in a desperate grip with one hand, he passed the other over her face, as if, in the absence of light, he might recognize something familiar in the sense of touch. She said, 'Thursday! You know me. I'm Bee.'

'Who's Bee?'

'We go to school together. We've known each other for years. We –' but she couldn't finish the sentence.

'You've come to take me away?'

'No! I've come to keep you here.'

'Where's here?'

'Our place. You know.'

'Our place?'

'You know. *Our* place,' Bee repeated.

'Why our place? What do we do here?'

It took all Bee's courage to say it. How do you say what matters more than anything else to you, to someone who seems not to be able to understand? How do you speak from the heart to someone who seems to have none? How can you remain human in the face of the inhuman? She tried more than once before it at last came out. 'We love each other.' At that he cried out again. He clasped her. Bee didn't know what he saw at that moment, she didn't know afterwards what she had seen. Had there been lights, had the sky split open with fire above them? Had the ground trembled, the world turned, shuddering on its side? Had there been a crack of thunder like a trumpet call? Had she felt, as she held him in her arms, taut and stiff and trembling, the piercing pain of his resistance to her love, had he writhed and changed and tried to escape her, had he fought, had he bruised, had he bitten her, in his agony? Had the mound in the corner of the bomb site opened up, had there been music, first the little fluting music of little people, the trampling of hundreds of tiny feet, the outcry of cheated

206

fantasy, the rumbling of an earth that opened to receive back into its depths the spirits who were contained within it? Had there been a song somewhere, triumphant and clear, like the floating melody of a solo trumpet, which said again and again that they had conquered? Had she really heard other voices than their own? All she could be certain of was the sudden knowledge that he was no longer fighting, but warm and gentle in her arms; that his cheek was against hers, his hair falling across her forehead, that he was holding her in arms that were kind and were glad to hold her. She felt, astonished and enlightened, his tears running down her face. Or was it just tears? The skies fell on them with warm, heavy drops of long awaited rain. It was very dark between the lightning flashes. They moved without speaking into the shelter of the brick arch, and sat underneath the heart scratched on the wall, still with their arms round each other. In spite of the clamour outside, the claps of thunder, metallic in their immediacy, Bee's eyelids were heavy, kept dropping. When they lifted of their own accord, she was astonished to find the storm over, the sky pale with the coming of the day. Thursday's head was heavy on her shoulder, but as she moved to stretch her cramped body, he woke and looked at her.

He said, 'Bee.'

'Thursday!'

There was a long pause.

'Are you all right?'

'I think so. Thursday. Are *you*?'

He said, surprised and joyful, 'I'm all right. Let's go home.'

CHAPTER TWENTY-ONE

ALTHOUGH it was almost day, the sky clear, with the uncertain colours of mother of pearl, when they reached Bee's home, the windows were bright with yellow electric light, the house the only one startlingly awake in the slumbering street. At the gate Bee stopped, and asked, 'What am I going to tell them?' But Thursday hadn't waited, seemed not to have heard. He had already raised the knocker and let it fall resoundingly on the door.

It was opened extraordinarily quickly by Bee's father. He said immediately, 'Where's Bee?'

'I'm here,' Bee said, joining Thursday on the doorstep. Her father turned back towards the kitchen door behind him and called out, 'She's back, Mum.' To Bee he said, 'You'd best come in,' and went in front of her, Bee following, uncomfortably. Thursday shut the front door and came last into the kitchen.

Mrs Earnshaw was sitting at the kitchen table, exactly as Bee had seen her sitting the afternoon before. She looked tired, much older, shadows under her eyes, her mouth a tight line, holding in all the things she wouldn't yet allow herself to say. She saw first Bee, then afterwards Thursday. Her eyes examined him, then came back to Bee again. Bee saw that she was very angry.

'You're back,' she said.

'Mum . . .'

'Do you know what time it is?'

Bee looked at the clock on the high mantelpiece. Its hands stood at half past four.

'Perhaps you'll tell me where you've been and what you've been doing?'

'I'm terribly sorry, Mum.'

'You can be sorry later. You tell me first where you've been.'

'Out,' Bee said, stupidly.

'I can see that, can't I? Out where?'

'I had to see Thursday.'

'What did you have to see Thursday for, may I ask?'

Bee hesitated, then said, 'I had to help him.'

'In the middle of the night? I said, in the middle of the night?'

'Yes,' Bee said.

'You ought to be ashamed of yourself. Coming home at this hour of the morning, tonight of all nights in the year.'

'It had to be Midsummer's ... Oh! You mean ... What happened to Jean?'

'A lot you thought about Jean and what she was going through when you went off on the sly. I'd never have thought it of you.'

'But what happened? Is she all right?'

'Jean's all right. Baby's all right too,' Bee's father said.

'Oh! A boy or a girl?'

'Boy. Trev's staying there with them.'

'You might have thought what it'd be like after the time we've had at the hospital, to come back and find you gone off without a word, no one knows where,' Mrs Earnshaw said.

'I'm sorry,' Bee said.

'You've got plenty to be sorry for I reckon,' her mother said.

'I've said I'm sorry, haven't I? What else do you want me to say?'

'I'd never have thought it of you. Thoughtless. Selfish. Wicked. I thought I could trust you.'

'What do you mean?' Bee asked.

'You spend the night out with a boy, and you come back and ask me, what do I mean?'

Thursday said, suddenly and surprisingly, 'She was making me safe.'

Mrs Earnshaw turned on him, 'So you've found your tongue, have you? Safe from what, I should like to know?'

'They wanted to keep me shut away,' Thursday said.

'It was for your own good they did it,' Mrs Earnshaw said.

Thursday cried out, 'No! They wouldn't let me . . .'

'Wouldn't let you what?' Mrs Earnshaw asked sharply.

Thursday said lamely, 'I had to be different. I was a different person. Nothing was real.'

'And Bee? Where does Bee come into this, then?'

'She knew which was really me,' he said.

'Was it you told Bee to come out to meet you this night?'

'No. I told him,' Bee said.

'Why couldn't you meet her in the daytime? Why didn't you come here and have it all open and above board?' Mrs Earnshaw said, still addressing Thursday.

'They wouldn't have let him,' Bee said.

'What do you say to that?' Bee's father said to Thursday.

'I didn't mean to hurt Bee,' Thursday said.

'Take Bee upstairs, Mum. I'll talk to Thursday down here,' Mr Earnshaw said. It was awful, Bee thought. It was like a bad play on telly, not like ordinary life. In a family you shouldn't have to talk to each other in separate rooms as if there were things too dreadful to be heard.

Upstairs in Bee's bedroom, she and her mother faced each other. Bee saw that the first tide of her mother's anger had turned. She was no longer just a rising voice, a wave of temper following great anxiety. She'd stopped, for the moment at least, saying all the unreasonable, angry things any mother would say to any erring child. Bee said quickly, 'Mum!'

'What?'

'You said sometimes you have to go against the rules.'

'What's that?'

'You said once, you can't always keep promises. You said sometimes you have to let people down you never thought you would. You said it was like that when your father had Lassie put away.'

'What's that got to do with now?'

'You said, you have to make up your own mind what's right to do.'

'You saying so it's all right if you stay out the night with a boy?'

'He isn't just a boy. He's Thursday!' Bee said, angry herself.

'A boy's a boy, however well you think you know him. I'd nothing against him until this, but this I will not have. Do you hear me?'

'Mum. You did say, sometimes you have to make up your own mind.'

'I may have. Go on.'

'It was like that last night. I knew you'd be angry . . .'

'You were right about that.'

'I had to get Thursday back!'

'Back from where? The hospital where he'd been put for his own good?'

'It wasn't for his own good! He was worse there.'

'You know more than the doctors. Is that it?'

'They didn't know what he was really like. They didn't know how he ought to be,' Bee said.

'What did you do for him they couldn't?'

'I knew that how he was in that hospital wasn't real.'

'Go on.'

'I had to see him somewhere else, where he could re-member.'

'Where's that?'

'Along Farmer's Lane,' Bee said reluctantly.

Bee's mother looked at her, then sat on the side of Bee's bed.

'Why there?'

'He liked it there,' Bee said.

There was another pause.

'What were you doing all that time?' Mrs Earnshaw asked.

'Thursday didn't come till after half past eleven. I was waiting for him.'

'And after he'd come?'

Bee was silent.

'What happened after, Bee?'

Bee said, 'Only I told him how I felt.'

'What do you mean?'

Bee almost told her everything. She wanted to be for-given, comforted, warmed by her mother's love, safe. But she saw suddenly that if she did this she would step back into childhood again. She would give up the right to make her own decisions and, what was more important, her own mistakes. She felt guilty and frightened, but she knew somewhere deep inside that she must keep a part of herself separate, secret, dark, unobserved, even from her mother. She said, 'I told him how much I minded.'

'Minded what?'

'About him?'

'That all, Bee?'

'Then there was the storm. There's a sort of place in a wall you can shelter in. We stopped there. I must have gone to sleep.'

'Him too?'

'Yes. That's why we didn't get back before.'

'Bee,' her mother said.

'Yes?' She hardened herself against further questions. There were some things she wasn't going to say. Like her mother had said, different people had different ways of seeing things, put different names to them. Bee saw now that she couldn't take someone else's naming, even from her mother. But Mrs Earnshaw didn't ask any more. She said, 'I don't know when I've been so tired. The baby wasn't born till just on half past two. Trev was with us most of the time. They wouldn't let him in with Jean. She had a bad time, poor lassie.'

'But she's really all right?' Bee asked.

'Aye. There was a time when they weren't sure. They came and told us things weren't going too well.'

'How awful for Trev,' Bee said.

'He's had a hard time these last days. Not that it's been easy just to look on and do nothing, either.'

'I'm sorry if I made it worse,' Bee made herself say.

'Not till tonight, you didn't,' her mother said.

'I'm sorry about that.'

'If you don't know what's right and what isn't after fifteen years, I reckon it's as much my fault as yours,' her mother surprisingly said. She lay back on Bee's pillow. 'I could do with a bit of a rest.'

'Tell me about the baby.'

'Dark. A long lad. Like your Dad.'

'And Jean?'

'Stephen Thomas, they're to call him. My Dad was Stephen. Don't know where they got the Thomas from.'

'It's nice. Aren't they terribly pleased?'

'Think it's never happened to anyone else.'

'How's Jean?'

There was a silence.

'Is Jean all right?' Bee asked, frightened. But when she looked at her mother, she saw why there had been no answer. Lying back on Bee's bed, exhausted, Mrs Earnshaw had been overtaken by the need for sleep. The shadows on her face were already lighter: she looked relaxed, younger, vulnerable. Bee looked at her with a curious mixture of feelings before she left the room and went downstairs.

'Is Jean all right, Dad?'

'She's fine. She's great. Bee, I'll fall over my own feet if I stay up any longer. I've to work today. Must get an hour's sleep if I can.'

Left alone in the kitchen, a table of used cups and plates between them, Bee and Thursday looked at each other.

'Tired?' Bee asked.

'Yes.'

'You've come a long way,' she said.

'It seemed like a minute or two. I didn't know it took so long,' he said.

'Time?'

'There wasn't any.'

'What was it like? Was it horrible?'

'Not all. Some of it was good. There was music. They liked my guitar. And singing. Different from here.'

'Sounds great,' Bee said, instantly jealous.

'It wasn't. It was sad, somehow.'

'Might you go back? Ever? Want to, I mean?'

He considered. 'It was easy there. Nobody asked you to decide anything. You weren't ever alone.'

'Then . . .?'

'Somehow it wasn't real.'

'Real?'

'Not like this. This kitchen. Your Mum and Dad.'

'They're real enough,' Bee said.

214

They still stood looking at each other. Thursday said suddenly, 'I brought you back something.' He put his hand in his pocket.

'What is it?' Bee asked.

'A thing. A sort of locket. There was always a lot of that sort of thing lying around. Anyone could have it.' His fingers opened, and shed the object into her palm.

'*What* is it?'

'Gold.'

Bee said, half in tears, 'Thursday, look!'

He looked. The thing in her hand shone yellow, heart shaped. He said, puzzled, 'I thought it was valuable. Something you could wear. I thought it was gold.'

Bee said, 'It's a leaf.'

'Nothing but a leaf?'

Bee said, 'It's a leaf. It's lived on a tree. There'll be other leaves. Because this one fell off, it doesn't mean there won't be more. There will be. Heaps of leaves. Like this one, but all different.'

'You mean, it's alive?'

Bee said, 'Gold would be exciting, but it doesn't do anything. I mean, you can buy things with it, but it's no use of itself. It isn't *real*.'

'What is real?' Thursday asked.

Bee thought, so quickly that her tongue couldn't have kept pace with her brain, of herself and Thursday holding each other in the clamour of the night; she thought of Jean, lying tired on her high white bed while a new person slept at the end of it; she thought of her mother and father, ordinary and everyday and homely, like this kitchen, and like stews and bread and washing up and homework; she thought of Antonia Codell singing out her belief in love; she thought of old Mrs Smith and her knowledge that Thursday could be saved. She thought of Lynne and of Hermia and of

Oberon and Puck, and of the hygienic hospital and the anxious young doctor; she thought of the willow herb on the bomb site, and of the young sliver of a moon which had seen them off it, not two hours ago. She thought of all these things in no time at all, and she knew that everything is only as real as it seems, and that how it seems to you at this one particular moment is all that you can judge it by, and that this is how you have to live. She said, 'I'll make you a cup of tea,' and saw Thursday sit at the crowded table, waiting for her to bring him the cup, as he'd sit and wait for her, for years that were still to come.

Some other Puffins you might enjoy

WHERE THE LILIES BLOOM
Vera and Bill Cleaver

'This is a fair land,' said the stranger, 'the fairest I have ever seen', and however impossible the tasks that were heaped upon her, Mary Call Luther never forgot his words. She had worries and responsibilities enough to make even a stalwart despair. There was her father coughing his life away, his grave already dug on a near-by mountain, a 'cloudy-headed' elder sister who would be dependent on her for life, and a smaller brother and sister still happy in their childish games of make-believe but needing food and clothing. How could she scrape a living together for them in this rough mountain country, so beautiful in spring and so bitterly cruel in winter?

It was a bleak, toilsome life, but even when sugar and shoe leather did become impossible luxuries, wasn't anything at all better than being parked in institutions?

THE TOMBS OF ATUAN
Ursula Le Guin

Arha was destined to be the One Priestess of the Nameless Ones of the Tombs of Atuan. As she grew up she learned the elaborate rituals of their service, the secrets of the Great Labyrinth that lay under the Tombs. And then one day, on her solitary wandering in the darkness, she discovered that someone *had* penetrated the deepest recesses of the maze. It was Ged, Wizard of Earthsea, seeking the lost half of the Ring of Erreth Akbe. Under the law of the Nameless Ones his violation of the Tombs means he must die, alone and enclosed in the blackness. But Arha rebels. Risking her own destruction, she keeps him as her private prisoner, telling no one, peering at him through her secret spy hole.

Gradually Ged wins her trust, offering her different values from the ones she has absorbed throughout her life, then together they share the terror, danger and dread which is necessary before the quest for the Ring of Erreth Akbe is completed.

THE CUCKOO TREE
Joan Aiken

'Fry that coachman!' said Dido, when there was a violent lurch and the coach turned over on its side. Then she started seeing to things, and there certainly was a lot to be seen to, for she and the injured Captain, as well as his secret, urgent dispatches, had been unceremoniously tipped into a hotbed of smugglers, witches, conspirators and cold-blooded murdering kidnappers, who all seemed to operate round a curiously shaped 'Cuckoo Tree'.

It would be silly of her devoted fans to wonder whether Dido really could save her two new friends, Chris and Tobit, from being cheated out of their birthright, rescue Captain Hughes from the spell he lay under, and save King Richard the Fourth from the Hanoverian plot to wreck his coronation, since she has somehow always achieved the impossible and managed to have a marvellous time doing it.

SOPHIA SCROOBY PRESERVED
Martha Bacon

'Are there any people in the world besides us?' Nono inquired of her ancient great-grandmother.

'What a thing to ask,' hissed Ami. 'Yes, there used to be some other people. Our people killed them all of course. We gave them to the hyenas. There aren't any more of them. Now get along before I put you in the pot.'

But there were other people, and they were dangerous too. It was lucky that Nona was so quick-witted and inquisitive, for her village was attacked and she fled into the bush to live like a wild thing. And this was to be only the beginning – she was taken across the Atlantic in a slave ship, sold to the gentle Scrooby family, given an education and a grand name, then sold again when the Scroobys were bankrupted.

All this would have been the end of any lesser character, but 'Sophia Scrooby' kept her wits and courage needle sharp, and emerged triumphantly unscathed.

A LONG WAY FROM VERONA
Jane Gardam

Set during the last War, this is Jessica Vye's own story about her own private battle to grow up in her own way, to live her own life in the confining world of a girls' day school and in the bleak little house her family had come to live in.

Sensitive, emotional and devastatingly truthful, Jessica steered her way past reef after reef, from a chance meeting with a maniac in some forbidden woods to an unbearable houseparty for children in a grand, snobbish household, her first disappointing love, and – eventually – her first success in life. For Jessica Vye is 'A Writer Beyond All Possible Doubt!' and at last she proves it conclusively, despite bad school essay marks, by winning a poetry competition in *The Times*.

This is a funny, gritty, and unsentimental book.

RED MOON AND BLACK MOUNTAIN
Joy Chant

It was only an ordinary bicycle ride at first – until the three children decided to follow a footpath across a meadow. Oliver went first. The faint path rippled in the haze and the cattle looked distorted and unreal. He drew a deep breath and went determinedly forward – then suddenly he was alone in another world, on a strange empty plain. Moments later a spear tore past his shoulder and stuck quivering in the ground. It was his introduction to a new life as one of a band of hunting and wandering tribesmen.

When he met Nicholas and Penelope again he hardly knew them, for he had become the Lord of Warriors, and his was the fearful honour of fighting the fallen Black Enchanter of the beautiful Star Magic, to save the Starlit Land from all his wickedness. And even when that bitter battle was done, Oliver found there was something more terrifying yet for him to endure.

EARLY THUNDER
Jean Fritz

It was 1774, and Daniel West's world was in a mess. Salem was his home, where people he knew were awaiting the punishment that was to come from England, because whatever England did about the Tea Party would affect the future of everyone.

The American War of Independence was coming closer and closer. The thunder was rolling now, and there was no telling when it would break into a storm, and life seemed blacker still to Daniel when he found his own loyalty wavering and his admired father disappointed him with an unexpected show of weakness.

Jean Fritz always involves us in matters of conscience as well as exciting historical periods, so that her books are not easily forgotten.

TRISTAN AND ISEULT
Rosemary Sutcliff

Long ago, in the days of warriors and heroes, Marc King of Cornwall rewarded Rivalin King of Lothian with the gift of his sister in marriage for the help he had given him in battle. Rivalin carried the princess joyfully back with him to his own land, and a year later they had a son. But the child was named Tristan, which means sorrow, for his mother left the world the day he entered it. Sixteen years afterwards, Tristan and his friends set out for Cornwall, little knowing what strange love and sorrow and tests of loyalty would be his in the land where he won Iseult of Ireland's love for himself, yet brought her back to be his uncle's Queen, weaving a story that would be sung and told throughout Europe for centuries to come.

This retelling of the old Celtic story is one of Rosemary Sutcliff's most memorable books, and one that pleases on many levels.